The kingdom of Montacroix has been described as a fantasyland. But to me, it's always been home. And while I've enjoyed the privileges of wealth, after my coronation my life will change.

It is, after all, one thing for the heir to the throne to be perceived as a playboy; it is quite another for the regent to be perceived that way. My father, determined that I marry, has been parading innumerable suitable prospects before me. Yet I remain determined to choose my own consort.

Although Sabrina Darling insists she isn't princess material, the American actress who haunts my dreams and torments my waking moments is most definitely a woman born to wear flowing silks and rich, disturbing scents. Sabrina is everything I've ever dreamed of in a woman, more than I'd hoped for in a bride.

And despite her claim that she no longer believes in fairy tales, I fully intend to make her my beloved wife. Forever.

Prince Burke Giraudeau de Montacroix

MEN at WORK

✈—MILLIONAIRE'S CLUB   🍎—BOARDROOM BOYS   🌼—MAGNIFICENT MEN

🐎—TALL, DARK & SMART   🩺—DOCTOR, DOCTOR   🔫—MEN OF THE WEST

⚙—MEN OF STEEL   🎖—MEN IN UNIFORM

MEN at WORK

JoAnn Ross

THE PRINCE & THE SHOWGIRL

MILLIONAIRE'S CLUB

Harlequin Books

TORONTO • NEW YORK • LONDON
AMSTERDAM • PARIS • SYDNEY • HAMBURG
STOCKHOLM • ATHENS • TOKYO • MILAN
MADRID • WARSAW • BUDAPEST • AUCKLAND

HARLEQUIN BOOKS
225 Duncan Mill Road, Don Mills,
Ontario, Canada M3B 3K9

ISBN 0-373-81039-3

THE PRINCE & THE SHOWGIRL

Dear Reader:

I'm delighted that *The Prince & The Showgirl*—my retelling of the classic legendary romance, *Cinderella*—has been chosen to be part of the MEN AT WORK series.

This is definitely not your mother's fairy tale. I couldn't resist tossing in a pinch of danger and intrigue to add spice to the story. Also, Sabrina's stepmother and stepsisters are worlds different from those original harridans.

And since Prince Burke Giraudeau de Montacroix is a very modern man, I knew he could fall in love only with a woman capable of slaying her own dragons.

Even with these changes, *The Prince & The Showgirl* (like all good fairy tales and Harlequin/Silhouette novels) does, of course, end with Prince Burke and Sabrina living happily ever after.

Which is, as always, my heartfelt wish for you.

JoAnn Ross

Don't miss any of our special offers. Write to us at the following address for information on our newest releases.
Harlequin Reader Service
U.S.: 3010 Walden Ave., P.O. Box 1325, Buffalo, NY 14269
Canadian: P.O. Box 609, Fort Erie, Ont. L2A 5X3

1

ONCE UPON A TIME, when she'd still believed in fairy tales, Sabrina Darling had fantasized about becoming a princess.

Instead of the hated thrift-store clothing she was forced to wear—worn and outdated outfits that inevitably drew taunts and jeers from her classmates, she would dress in richly colored flowing silks that whispered as she walked, sparkling glass slippers and a gleaming gold-filigree crown studded with priceless diamonds, emeralds and rubies.

Although Sabrina had always been an imaginative child, the princess fantasies, which she had indulged in for as long as she could remember, began in earnest shortly after her eighth birthday. That was the year her mother died.

Sabrina had never known her father. Her mother, Melody, had divorced him before Sabrina was born. Bitter over various grievances—some real, others imagined—Melody had not told her young husband— a struggling country singer and songwriter—that he was about to become a father.

Such short-sighted stubbornness resulted in mother and daughter living in near poverty in San Antonio. Unfortunately, lack of funds hadn't kept Melody out of the honky-tonks; after all, she was pretty and young and there was always some man willing and eager to buy her a drink. Or two. Or more.

Then, late one night on a cold, rainy December, unhappy fate caught up with Melody. On her way home from a local cowboy bar, she had the misfortune to be a passenger in an oil rigger's metallic blue Thunderbird that rolled over on the interstate outside of town.

The car was totaled. The kindly highway patrolman who'd broken the news to Sabrina had assured her that her mother had died instantly.

"Don't worry, sugar," he'd soothed, "your mama didn't suffer none."

And that was the reason Sabrina ended up in a cramped trailer on the outskirts of Waco, Texas, with her grandmother, a disapproving harridan who found a naturally spirited young girl difficult to deal with.

Wretchedly unhappy and forlorn, Sabrina passed most of the next year escaping into her bright, sparkling world of daydreams.

She spent long lonely hours desperately wishing for a fairy godmother to suddenly appear and, with one wave of her sparkling magic wand, transform her miserable life.

While the rest of her third-grade class was struggling to learn long division, Sabrina would lose herself in romantic daydreams. Her favorite one had the classroom door suddenly burst open. Prince Charming would ride in astride his magnificent white steed, sweep her up behind him and carry her off at a heady gallop to his castle. A dazzling palace with turrets and towers that pierced the sky. And a moat.

Of course it went without saying that she and her handsome prince would live happily ever after.

On the first anniversary of her mother's death, her grandmother decided to call Nashville, Tennessee, and instructed Sabrina's father to come and fetch his daughter. It was time father and daughter got to know each other.

Sabrina had been stunned to learn that Sonny Darling was her father. Why, he was famous. More than famous, he was a star! She watched him all the time on television, singing on the stage of the Grand Ole Opry, exchanging quips with Minnie Pearl.

But never once had she imagined that the man on the television was the man her mother had always talked about so disparagingly.

When Sonny showed up at the trailer, looking strong and rich and incredibly handsome in his black Western-cut suit and silver-tipped ostrich-skin boots, he embodied the prince in all Sabrina's escapist daydreams.

She was welcomed into her new Nashville home—a huge white pillared Georgian mansion reminiscent of antebellum days—by Dixie, Sonny's pretty red-haired wife.

In no time she'd inherited two new parents, two half sisters and a new and famous last name. But deep down inside, Sabrina never quite outgrew a need to prove to her father that she was worth saving.

MAYBE THAT'S WHY, nineteen years later, she was standing on the deck of a sleek white boat speeding toward a castle, halfway around the world in the principality of Montacroix.

From a distance, the palace rising up from the island in the middle of the lake appeared to be a many-towered Camelot. Its wedding-cake spires pierced the silver mist, gleaming like polished alabaster in the golden shafts of sunlight. It could have served as the inspiration for her long-ago daydreams.

"Oh!" breathed Ariel Darling, Sabrina's half sister.

The lake wind ruffled the pleated miniskirt of Ariel's robin's egg blue designer suit, revealing the long, coltish legs that had made her famous as a vamp on a popular daytime soap opera.

"It always affects people that way," the man piloting the boat said when he heard Ariel's sharp intake of breath.

"It's like something from a fairy tale," Raven said, gazing at the edifice across the diamond-bright waters of Lake Losange. At thirty, Raven was the middle of the three Darling sisters.

"That's what they all say," he agreed amiably. "Especially Americans. We Europeans are more blasé about our palaces, since we've got them scattered all over the place."

Sabrina remained silent, staring at the enchanting sun-gilded vision. The Montacroix royal palace was like a dazzling jewel set in the very center of the lake's sapphire waters.

The fact it was inhabited by the Giraudeau regents, the most talked-about European lineage, made it all the more glamorous.

Something stirred in Sabrina. Some lingering fanciful emotion she recognized as intrinsically dangerous. Frowning, she folded her arms across the front of her scarlet satin baseball jacket.

The boatman's dark eyes, beneath his cap, took a quick tour of Sabrina's alluring looks—her gleaming golden blond hair, flowing from a red, white and blue sequined baseball cap all the way down to her waist and her attractive legs encased in over-the-knee, lace-up red suede boots.

"Are you ladies friends of Prince Burke?"

Last month's *People* magazine had referred to Burke Giraudeau as the world's most eligible bachelor. And now, with his upcoming coronation, he was even more in demand. From the boatman's overtly masculine appraisal, Sabrina suspected that he was viewing her sisters and her as three more females determined to capture the prize.

"Hardly," Sabrina said dryly. From what she'd read of Prince Burke's life-style—polo playing in Monaco, skiing in the French Alps, photographing endangered species in Kenya, and Grand Prix auto racing all over the world—she was certain that she wouldn't like such a self-indulgent man.

Her twenty-eight years had taught her a few things—and one of them was that she had no interest in a man who was obviously nothing more than an international playboy.

Then, again, she couldn't help feeling smug about the fact she'd be performing in front of a real prince for the first time....

"Then you must be a friend of Princess Noel's," the man probed a little deeper.

"We've never met."

"Perhaps you know Princess Chantal. Her husband's an American, you know," he offered, as if hoping to encourage a more detailed response.

"I know," Sabrina answered with blatant disinterest.

Her mind still on the errant playboy prince, she didn't bother to add that she'd met the princess when she and her sisters had performed at the Kennedy Center in Washington, D.C. She'd found her to be a warm and gracious person.

Ariel shot Sabrina a mildly rebuking look and said, "We're here to perform for the coronation."

"Not exactly the coronation," Raven corrected. She pushed a cloud of jet black hair from her face. The wind picked up; pewter clouds gathered overhead.

"Actually, we've been booked to sing for the public festival the day before the coronation. And Princess Chantal's fund-raiser." The gala event, staged to raise funds for the princess's favorite charity—the Rescue the Children Fund—was definitely a professional coup.

The man's eyes lighted with recognition. "Then that would make you the Little Darlings."

"We dropped the *Little* years ago," Sabrina said. Her tone was unnecessarily sharp, earning her warning glances from both sisters and her mother.

"My daughters prefer to call themselves simply The Darlings now that they've grown up," Dixie divulged. Her honeyed Southern accent turned as thick as molasses in an obvious attempt to soothe the man's injured feelings. "Do you have daughters, *monsieur?*"

"Two," he mumbled.

"Then I'm sure you'll understand how sensitive some young girls are," Dixie soothed, placing a hand on his beefy arm.

Sabrina had always thought of her stepmother as a velvet bulldozer, especially when she pulled out her Southern belle routine. Dixie's behavior was every bit as obvious as Scarlett's had been when she'd put on those drapes and gone to entice Rhett into giving her money. Transparent it might be. But it never failed to work. And this time was no exception.

The boatman looked down at Dixie's black suede glove. Color flooded into his already ruddy cheeks, like a spreading fever.

"That I do, *madame*," he acknowledged. "When my oldest girl, Gabriella, turned sixteen, she instructed her mother and me never to call her Gabby again. Wasn't 'sophisticated,' she said." He scowled at the memory.

"Daughters." Dixie sighed commiseratingly, patting

his thick arm. "They can be a trial at times. But they're also such a blessing. We parents have no choice but to put up with their little moods. Isn't that so?"

Muttering his agreement in the French of his country, the boatman pulled the craft up to the slip. By the time he'd helped all four women onto the floating wooden dock, the wounded-puppy look was gone, revealing that Dixie Darling had made yet another conquest.

PRINCE BURKE Giraudeau de Montacroix was not in a good mood. He paced the floor of the palace library in long strides, the heels of his riding boots clacking on the two-hundred-year-old marble flooring.

"This is ridiculous," he spat out, slicing the air with his leather crop. Frustration was etched on the planes of his lean, intelligent face. "I shall not allow a few malcontents to make me a prisoner in my own home."

Burke's dark eyes flashed with a temper he usually managed to control. He raked his hand through his thick hair and stopped his pacing in front of the George V desk.

"A Giraudeau does not run from trouble like some frightened coward," he reminded the older man seated behind the gleaming expanse of mahogany.

Prince Eduard Giraudeau, Burke's father and regent—for another ten days—of the European principality, displayed his own frustration. "I am not calling you a coward," he bellowed, lowering his voice only when he realized he might be heard by a servant hovering outside the library door. Ever since the warnings had begun appearing around the country, gossip had run amok.

"And I understand your dislike of the situation. But

we cannot take for granted the assumption that these are merely malcontents."

The elder prince was playing with an ivory-handled letter opener that had once belonged to Bonaparte. From his glower, Burke suspected that his father would love to thrust Napoleon's gold blade into the leader of the so-called insurrectionist group's black heart.

"I will not risk the life of my only son—and the future of this country—merely because you do not wish to be inconvenienced," Eduard insisted.

It took an effort, but Burke managed not to shoot back that what his father was suggesting was far from mere inconvenience. On the contrary, it was a great deal closer to house arrest.

"Caine?" He turned toward his brother-in-law, who'd been sitting silently in a chair across the room, watching the argument that had been raging for the past half hour. "What do you think?"

It was not an idle question. An American hero who'd earned a medal for throwing himself in front of his president, subsequently taking a bullet from a would-be assassin's gun, Caine had been a top member of the president's security force. Indeed, he'd met Chantal, his wife and Burke's sister, when he'd been assigned—against his wishes—to provide protection for her during an American tour two years ago.

At the time, threats had been made against Princess Chantal's life, and although she refused to take them seriously, fortunately Caine had. Weeks after saving her life, he'd opened up a Washington, D.C., security business with his partner, then arrived in Montacroix and proposed to the beautiful headstrong princess. She'd almost given up on convincing the handsome security agent that they were meant to be together.

Burke's father was well-known for his tendency to allow his heart to rule his head where his family was concerned. When Chantal had nearly been killed in a deliberately set fire, Prince Eduard had actually demanded that the Montacroix legislature bring back the guillotine.

Fortunately the august legislators had resisted the prince's orders and eventually Eduard had relented, settling for imprisonment instead. He had, however, been heard to say on numerous occasions that he wished the dungeon prison cells were still available for the miscreants' incarceration.

"I think," Caine said, rubbing his chin as he carefully measured his words, "that right now you remind me of your sister. She almost got herself killed by refusing to acknowledge the fact that she was in danger." His expression was grave, his eyes dark with concern.

Burke muttered a low harsh curse in his native French. "This so-called independence movement is nothing but a bunch of trouble-causing idiots. Crackpots, as you Americans call them."

"They may be crackpots," Caine allowed. "But according to my sources at Interpol, they're heavily armed. And believe me, Burke, there is nothing more dangerous than a maniac with an automatic weapon."

Trusting his brother-in-law's judgment even as he detested his undoubtedly accurate opinion, Burke flung himself into a flimsy Louis XIV chair. His hands curled tightly around the gold-leaf arms, and for a long silent time, he glowered down at his boot tips.

"What would you suggest I do? Keeping in mind," he tacked on quickly, "that I will not give the people of Montacroix the impression that their future regent is a weakling."

"I doubt anyone would think that," Caine responded mildly. "Besides, despite this little cell of miscreants, all the polls show that the majority of citizens like your family. And ninety-eight percent of them would rather remain a monarchy than return rule of Montacroix to France.

"And," he added, "although no one's polled them on this question, I also know that they'd rather have a live monarch who was sensible enough to be cautious than a dead hero."

"Isn't that what I've been telling you?" Prince Eduard broke in.

Burke shrugged. "Life is always a risk," he pointed out. "Especially for those who are perceived to possess wealth."

"All the more reason to tilt the odds in your favor," Caine countered.

Knowing when he'd been bested, Burke threw back his head and laughed. "Now I remember why I never play chess with you, Caine." A bit more relaxed, he leaned forward, linked his fingers between his knees and said, "So what do you have in mind?"

"Your father has a good point about increasing the guards," Caine said. "We've also begun a background check on all the palace employees."

Burke's dark brows crashed downward toward his nose. "You are investigating the staff?"

"The way to catch a criminal, whether he's an international terrorist or a run-of-the-mill neighborhood thug, is to think like one. If I wanted to kill you, Burke, the first thing I'd try to do is place someone on the inside."

Remembering how Chantal had almost died in a fire set by a stand-in waiter at a Philadelphia dinner party, Burke silently conceded that point. "What else?"

"You need bodyguards."

"I refuse."

"So did Chantal, in the beginning. Which is why your father and the president came up with that cock-amamy idea of me pretending to be an assistant secretary of state. But later she was damned glad to have me hanging around."

For a great deal more than reasons of security, Caine remembered, opting not to share the intimate particulars of their romance with his wife's brother and father.

"I will accept one bodyguard. No more," Burke said. Diplomacy and compromise, he reminded himself, were at times a necessity. He would give in to his father and Caine on this point, winning a more important one down the line.

"You need at least three," Prince Eduard insisted.

"One." Burke gave his father a strong, no-nonsense look. "And I am only permitting this in order to lessen your concerns."

"You are a very stubborn man," Eduard muttered.

Burke's lips curved in a faint smile. "I had a very good teacher," he said mildly. "What else?" he asked, turning back to Caine.

"We'll want plainclothes people dispersed through the crowd the day of the festival. Along with a visible uniformed detail."

Burke shrugged. "No problem. I would not want any innocent civilians to be injured by these rabble-rousers."

"And, although you are the target, we should put guards on Chantal, Noel, and your mother, to prevent them from being used to get to you."

"You mean as hostages?" That unpalatable idea had not occurred to Burke.

"It's been known to happen."

"Definitely the women shall be assigned bodyguards," Burke said with a decisiveness that Caine suspected would serve him well when he ascended to the throne.

Caine did not want to consider how Chantal would react when she learned that she was about to be put under protection again. It didn't matter how angry she got, he decided. Because he would do anything to keep his wife safe.

"Can you take care of this?" Burke asked Caine.

"I already have. There's one thing more."

Burke frowned. "If it's about the race—"

"A Grand Prix event is dangerous enough by itself," Caine interrupted. "Add to that the possibility of someone tampering with your car and you're just asking for trouble."

Burke shook his dark head. "I will not cancel the race. The Montacroix Grand Prix has been the most glamorous in the European racing circuit for more than fifty years. The race is an important tourist draw. Why, for the past two years, we have hosted more spectators than Monaco."

"We are not asking you to cancel anything," Prince Eduard said. "There is no reason that the race cannot continue as scheduled."

Burke was on his feet again. "Neither will I forfeit. I have every intention of winning."

"Winning isn't everything." Caine regretted having said the words the moment he heard them leave his mouth. In many ways, he and his brother-in-law were a great deal alike; Caine had never responded well to worn clichés and knew Burke didn't either.

"Since I've always admired you, Caine," Burke said, "I will pretend I did not hear that." He folded his arms across the front of his white shirt. "I intend to race. The people expect it of me. Indeed, without meaning to sound immodest, my participation is one of the reasons the Montacroix Grand Prix has become so successful in past years."

Burke had realized long ago that many of the people showed up out of some dark, slightly warped anticipation, hoping to watch him crash. But money was money, after all, and a lot of it flowed into Montacroix's coffers during the annual event.

"I also have every intention of winning. This one point is not negotiable."

Having spent the past two years intimately living with a gorgeous example of Giraudeau tenacity, Caine had learned to recognize when he was licked.

"If we can't change your mind, we'll at least want our own people in the pits."

"Fine." Having gotten his way on this major point, Burke decided he could afford to be generous. "So long as they don't get in the way."

"They won't."

Caine stood as well. "Well then, I guess I'd better get to work."

"Thank you, Caine," Prince Eduard said. "Once again our family is indebted to you for your assistance."

"I just hope I can be of help, sir," Caine said.

"Of that I have no doubt," the regent responded. "Oh, and please tell my daughter that her mother and I would like the entire family at dinner this evening. We will be having guests."

"Guests?" Burke asked suspiciously.

As the coronation had grown closer, his father had begun engaging in embarrassingly overt matchmaking. There had been several times over the past six months when Burke had innocently entered the dining room, only to find another candidate—usually some winsome European princess—smiling enticingly up at him.

Burke knew that his father's heavy-handed match-making had one goal: to ensure an heir. Burke realized that some day he would have to marry. It was, after all, his duty. In the meantime, he was enjoying his single life.

"That singing group Chantal recommended for the festival," his father reminded him. "The Darlings."

"Oh." Burke had forgotten. "The daughters of that country singer who recently died." An image immediately came to mind: one of women wearing beaded, fringed cowgirl outfits and high, towering platinum hair sprayed to a rock-hard consistency.

"That's right," Eduard agreed. "Since the young women and their mother have come a very long way to perform, we must extend a warm welcome. Your mother has invited them to stay here at the palace," he revealed. "We will, of course, expect you at dinner, as well."

Personally, Burke thought that the women's long trip hadn't exactly been a sacrifice. Not when you considered what performing at the precoronation festival could do to their careers. Still, knowing his mother's feelings about hospitality, he realized that tonight's dinner was a command performance.

"I'll be there," he agreed, deciding that he'd just have to test his car's new engine earlier in the day than planned.

"Of course you will," Prince Eduard agreed, obviously not having expected any other answer.

At that moment the phone on his desk rang. As he answered it, Burke and Caine left the library.

For a man who could afford to purchase whatever in the world might strike his fancy, there was one thing that was extremely difficult for Burke to obtain: privacy.

And now, thanks to a noisy, undoubtedly impotent group of malcontents, he'd just lost a bit more.

As he strode across the brick driveway, headed toward the garage, Burke's scowl mirrored the threatening clouds gathering overhead.

Despite the enviable fact that he would soon ascend to the throne of one of Europe's richest—albeit smallest—countries, Prince Burke Giraudeau de Montacroix was definitely not a happy man.

IN THE LIBRARY of a baronial estate a mere five kilometers from the Giraudeau palace, a cadre of well-dressed gentlemen sat in priceless antique chairs, sipping hundred-year-old cognac while discussing the upcoming coronation.

One silver-haired man, the owner of the estate, stood. "My friends, we are living in exciting times. In a mere ten days, that upstart Prince Burke will have been eliminated, allowing the principality of Montacroix, after nearly two-hundred long years, to finally be returned to its rightful owner."

He lifted his Baccarat balloon glass. *"Vive la France."*

Outside the leaded glass windows, a roll of thunder echoed ominously on the horizon.

The other five men stood and raised their own glasses. *"Vive la France,"* they echoed as a jagged line of sulfurous lightning streaked across the darkening sky.

2

THE NARROW ROAD from the palace twisted like a corkscrew through the woods. Snowcapped mountains rose in the distance; dark green pine trees scented the air.

"It says here," Dixie read aloud from her travel guide, "that Montacroix was purchased by the Giraudeau family from the French government after Napoleon's disastrous Russian campaign."

They were in a gray limousine currently winding its way through the thick forest. The liveried driver had greeted them politely, stashed what luggage he could in the massive trunk, arranged with the boatman to have the rest delivered to the palace, then demonstrated the limo's various accoutrements: television, telephone, a bar and even a VCR.

Having ridden in limousines many times before, Sabrina refused to be impressed by the trappings of royalty. Still, the snowy orchids blooming in crystal vases on either side of the back doors were a nice touch, she admitted.

"Apparently France was nearly broke from funding the wars and had begun selling off land to local noblemen to replenish its treasury," Dixie read.

"Well, I can certainly identify with that," Sabrina muttered, thinking back to the devastating day of her father's funeral.

Everyone who was anybody in the country music

business had turned out to say goodbye to Sonny Darling. Every hotel and motel in town had been booked for what had become Nashville's social event of the year.

Fans from all corners of the world sent flowers. When local florists ran out of blooms, florists from as far away as Memphis had been enlisted to help fill the telegraphed orders. Floral arrangements, ranging from the overly elaborate to the sweetly simple, filled the chapel.

Sonny Darling's name was legend, known even to those who'd never tuned their car radios to a country station.

The seventh son of a seventh son, Sonny had been born into a sharecropping family in Alabama. When he was five years old, he'd joined the rest of his family in the fields picking cotton and peanuts. Since there wasn't any money for birthday presents, for Sonny's sixth birthday his father had taken a wooden cigar box and a copper coil from a rusting old car and fashioned a crude, but workable guitar.

That simple instrument was to prove the turning point in young Sonny's life. By age ten, he was singing and plucking in the streets for pocket money. Although his road to success had been a rocky one, by the time he was thirty-three, he'd performed at the White House and was a featured regular on the Grand Ole Opry before winning his own weekly television variety show. That was the same year Sabrina had been rescued from her ill-tempered grandmother; and before she could get used to the idea that she even had a father, let alone such a famous one, she found herself appearing on the television show with Ariel and Raven, Sonny's other daughters. Billed as the Little Darlings, they had appeared on the show for five memorable years.

And then, he was gone. Without warning, his heart had simply stopped when he was onstage at the Celebrity Theater in Phoenix, singing the second verse of his latest megahit, "Here Comes Trouble Again."

As stricken as she had been by her father's sudden death, Sabrina had managed to find some comfort in the fact that he'd died doing what he'd always loved best.

Hand-lettered signs of support and grief and encouragement had been held up as the limousine left the cemetery. Alone for the first time since they'd received the news, Dixie had taken the opportunity to drop her bombshell: Sonny had died owing a virtual fortune in ten years' worth of back taxes to the IRS.

Apparently the accountant had filled out all the forms, and Dixie and Sonny had believed they always paid right on time. But according to the hateful little man from the IRS, Sonny's manager had embezzled the money for himself, using it to pay off his gambling debts. This was the man the girls had always called "Uncle Dan," the same man who'd been their father's best friend since Sonny's early days in Nashville, when he'd spent every waking hour trudging up and down Music Row, trying to push his tapes on anyone who'd listen.

Naturally Sonny's daughters offered to help. Raven expressed disappointment that all she could get her hands on was a few thousand. A successful producer of music videos, she'd recently tied up her funds buying a studio in downtown Atlanta.

Ariel, who lived comfortably in the flats of Beverly Hills, had offered to sell her racing-green Jaguar convertible. Like her famous father, she tended to spend more money than she saved, so, despite the generous salary she received from the television soap opera, her bank account was nothing to brag about.

Sabrina also lacked savings. Divorced from one of Broadway's brightest and most successful playwrights, she had learned the hard way what happened when a starry-eyed prospective bride failed to read her prenuptial agreement.

When her six-year marriage had broken up last spring, her former husband had ended up with almost everything, and Sabrina had left the marriage the same way she'd come into it—nearly broke with only the clothes on her back. But a great deal wiser.

Although the recession had hit Broadway, along with the rest of the country, she managed to find steady work in commercials and public service announcements, with an occasional short-run so far off Broadway as to be in other states. And while it definitely wasn't Shakespeare, it paid the rent. Most of the time.

After thanking her daughters for their generosity, Dixie had tearfully gone on to say that their proffered help wouldn't be enough. Because according to her new accountant, after she sold the thoroughbred horses that had been Sonny's pride and joy, and the farm, and all Sonny's cars and paintings, the IRS debt came to a staggering three million dollars. Plus change.

Raven, the businesswoman in the group, had immediately advised Dixie to declare bankruptcy.

But Dixie had just as quickly rejected that suggestion, refusing to tarnish her husband's reputation.

But they weren't to worry, she had insisted with renewed strength. Because she had a plan.

Silence had settled over the funeral-home limo like a shroud. Dixie finally broke it, professing that there was only one answer: the girls should record an album. And go on tour to promote it.

As stunned as Sabrina had been by that idea—after all, it had been years since she and her sisters had sung together publicly—Sabrina had known that it was not her own livelihood Dixie had been worried about. It was Sonny's reputation. Something Dixie had guarded over the years with all the ferocity of a mother bear. And so, by the time they had reached the Colonial-Williamsburg-style Opryland Hotel, Sonny Darling's daughters had reluctantly agreed to their mother's proposal. Just as Dixie had always known they would.

The storm that had been threatening finally arrived; the gray skies over Montacroix opened up. Sabrina watched the raindrops streak down the window of the limousine weaving through the mist-bound trees on its way to the palace.

"The principal industries are tourism and banking," Dixie continued to read, pulling Sabrina out of her reverie, "along with a steady growth in wine production. The per capita income is among the highest in the world, and taxes are among the lowest."

No one answered. The truth was, none of them were really listening all that closely to their mother. They'd grown accustomed to her ongoing travelogues. Indeed, taking a driving vacation with Dixie always took twice as long as originally planned because they were continually having to stop at some local tourist site. Sonny had always joked that Dixie had never met a historical marker she didn't like.

The limousine turned the corner and suddenly the woods gave way to a rolling expanse of dewy velvet the brilliant green of Oz's Emerald City. A yellow sign, posted along the side of the narrow, curving road, announced a peacock crossing. Dark, glossy animals rustled in topiary gardens, seemingly disciplined by the precise hand of a sculptor.

Formal gardens were ablaze with roses, rhododendrons, oleanders and magnolias, and the terra-cotta urns flanking the curving pathways were spilling over with colorful blossoms of crimson, mauve, salmon, pink, yellow and white. "It reminds me of Fantasyland," Ariel murmured.

"The book describes Montacroix as a place where fantasy and reality meld together as they do nowhere else in the world," Dixie agreed. "Oh, this is interesting."

"What's that?" Sabrina asked distractedly.

It was happening again; she could feel herself falling under the spell of an enchanting scene that could have been born in her dreams. She would not have been the least bit surprised if a horse-drawn gilt carriage had suddenly pulled through the elaborately stylized wrought-iron gates, carrying a fairy-tale princess on her way to the ball.

"Succession to the Montacroix throne is through the male line. If any succeeding prince fails to produce an heir, title to the principality reverts to France."

"That is interesting," Raven agreed.

"I wonder if that means Prince Burke is in the market for a bride," Ariel mused. "Boy, it sure would solve all our financial problems if one of us got lucky!"

Dixie and Raven laughed at the outrageous suggestion. Sabrina, gazing out the rain-streaked window, failed to comment.

THEY'D REACHED THE PALACE. The driver pulled the car beneath the porte cochere. Dark green ivy climbed up the walls, red and white rosebushes flanked the cobblestone path. Nearby towering poplars shaded aged white stone.

A pair of footmen, carrying enormous black umbrellas, hurried to open the limousine doors, ushering them indoors. The entry hall resembled an enormous stage set. Graceful Ionic columns fashioned from black-veined gold marble lined the walls. The floor was paved with black marble; a crystal chandelier dripped golden light from the domed ceiling where chubby-cheeked cherubs frolicked across an ancient fresco; Renaissance Flemish tapestries woven in silk and gold threads shared wall space with ornately framed portraits of Giraudeau ancestors.

"Well, we're definitely not in Kansas anymore," Sabrina murmured.

The words had no sooner left her mouth than a woman appeared, descending the curving stairway. Having discovered at a young age that clothes were theater, Princess Chantal Giraudeau de Montacroix had developed her own style, a dramatic image that enabled her, even when wearing a simple silk blouse and jeans, to steal the show without even trying.

Today she was wearing a scarlet silk blouse that set off her dark hair and eyes, and a pair of white silk trousers. The famed Giraudeau rubies flashed warmly at her ears.

"Dearest Dixie," Chantal greeted them with outstretched hands and genuine warmth. "Raven. Ariel. And dear Sabrina. Don't you all look wonderful!"

The ultraglamorous princess who had once kept an entire army of tabloid paparazzi working overtime to keep up with her jet-set life-style, brushed cheeks with each woman in turn, enveloping them in a cloud of perfume.

"*Bonjour*. How grand to see you all again! Everyone

has so been looking forward to your arrival. Unfortunately, *Maman* is in Paris for the afternoon with Noel—a charity event—and asks that I extend her apologies for not being here to greet you personally.

"And Caine, Burke and my father have locked themselves away in the library. Something to do with the coronation, I suppose, but Caine is being frustratingly closemouthed about everything. So I am afraid that I represent the entire welcoming committee."

"You're more than enough, Princess," Dixie said. Her daughters seconded her statement.

"I do hope you had a pleasant journey," Chantal said conversationally.

"The flight was long," Dixie answered. "But the movie was good. It was a Mel Gibson film, and although I couldn't hear a word of dialogue through the plastic earphones, I did enjoy the action."

"And of course watching Mel Gibson is always a treat," Ariel added with a wicked feminine grin reminiscent of her siren daytime character.

"That is so true," Chantal agreed with a smile. "Mel's a long-time friend of the family. He's been invited to the coronation."

Her smile brightened, lighting up her remarkable gypsylike dark eyes. "I'll introduce you," she told Ariel. "You two can talk shop."

"Dear Lord, the plane must've crashed over the Atlantic," Ariel said on a long, dramatic sigh. "Because it's obvious that I've died and gone to heaven."

Chantal laughed. "You must be exhausted. Let me show you to your rooms."

"It's very generous of you to invite us to stay in the palace," Dixie said.

"It's very generous of you to take time away from your busy tour to perform for Burke's festivities,"

Chantal countered. "As I told you when we met in Washington, it was beginning to look as if we'd end up with a group of stuffy old chamber musicians. Not that chamber music isn't quite pleasant, in its place," she amended.

"Unfortunately, my father, bless his heart, can be quite old-fashioned and more than a little rigid. It took a great deal of persuasion to convince him that times had changed since his own coronation."

They followed the princess up the long, ornate curving staircase, down a long hall carpeted in priceless Persian rugs. More nameless ancestors, trapped for eternity in their gilded frames, gazed down from the wall.

"Perhaps you should have started out giving him a rap tape to listen to," Sabrina suggested. "That way we would have sounded mild by comparison."

Chantal stopped and treated Sabrina to another one of her famous smiles that had appeared on magazine covers all over the world. "What a *merveilleuse* idea! I do wish that I'd thought of it." Then she surprised them with a wink that was worlds away from the glamorous jet-set princess of the tabloids. "Fortunately, *Maman* is very persuasive."

She stopped in front of a door at the end of the hallway. "I do hope this will be adequate."

The suite was a great deal more than adequate. The sitting room alone was three times the size of Sabrina's entire SoHo apartment.

Her appreciative gaze swept the vast room, taking in the dramatic red silk wall coverings, the crimson roses blooming on the needlepoint carpet. The arched mullion windows were framed in white Belgium lace; that same lace adorned the French doors leading out to the balcony. Both the windows and the white wrought-iron balcony allowed a splendid view of Lake Losange, now draped in a soft, silvery mist.

A welcoming fire blazed in an intricately carved marble fireplace. On a nearby marble-topped table there was a basket of fresh fruit, cheeses, boxes of water crackers and a crystal bowl of caviar nestled on sparkling ice chips. Nearby, wine and bottles of mineral water had also been put on ice, by an unseen servant.

"It's stunning," Sabrina said when she found her voice again. Although the Darlings had been considered wealthy in Nashville, she was beginning to realize that Sonny's annual royalties, as generous as they'd been, probably wouldn't even pay the household expenses on this palace.

Princess Chantal, Sabrina decided, could undoubtedly pay off Sonny's entire tax bill with her weekly clothing allowance.

Sabrina's mother and sisters, appearing a little shell-shocked themselves, murmured their own admiration of the suite.

"There are four bedrooms," Chantal said, waving a beringed hand toward a pair of doors. "Two on this side of the sitting room and an additional two on the other. They both have their own bathrooms, of course, and you'll undoubtedly be pleased to know that the plumbing is modern.

"Monique will be in momentarily to tend to your luggage. She'll be your maid while you are staying in the palace. Although she's young, she comes from a good family. I believe you'll be pleased."

Their own personal maid. Sabrina knew that Ariel would absolutely love the idea. So would Dixie. And even possibly, Raven. Sabrina, always independent, did not. But not wanting to offend Chantal, she kept her opinion to herself, vowing simply to unpack her clothes herself.

"Dinner is served at eight. The family's very eager to meet you, of course, but if you'd prefer, trays will be sent up from the kitchen."

"Of course we'll eat with the family," Dixie said quickly, answering for her daughters, who did not protest.

"*Bien*. It is our custom to have cocktails in the library before dinner. Since the palace has a great many twists and turns, and I would hate for you to get lost your first night here, Caine and I will be at your door at seven-thirty.

"In the meantime, if there is anything you wish— anything at all—Monique will be happy to get it for you."

Twenty minutes later, after sharing some cheese and crackers with the others, Sabrina was wandering around her spacious bedroom, examining the antique furniture that, while centuries old, revealed signs of tender loving care. A high canopied poster bed draped in diaphanous white gauze took up much of the room.

Walking over to the window, she sipped her wine— a crisp, dry sauvignon blanc from the Giraudeau vineyards—and gazed out at the enchanting, mist-draped view below.

In the distance, near the lake, she caught a glimpse of something red streaking through the trees. A closer inspection revealed it to be a race car, tearing around the curves at neck-breaking speed.

Undoubtedly the playboy prince, Sabrina decided. Her lips drew into a disapproving frown even as she found herself unable to drag her gaze away from the dangerous sight.

THE CAR HANDLED like a dream. Burke guided the sleek Formula One racing Ferrari around the tight curves, pleased when it responded to the lightest touch.

He had not been bragging when he'd told his father and brother-in-law that he would win the race this year; arrogance was not Burke's style. But he was confident. And he'd been working toward this goal for the past five years.

Like so many other rulers-in-waiting, Burke had been forced to practice patience until his father relinquished power. Not that he hadn't found plenty to keep himself occupied in the meantime. He oversaw the tourist council, which was an important sector of his country's economy, served as chairman of the board of the Giraudeau Bank, and was active in promoting sports.

He'd become captain of the Montacroix polo team specifically to draw more of the international horse set to his country. He had succeeded. During the season, the narrow cobblestone streets were packed with European luxury cars parked bumper to gleaming bumper.

His Grand Prix racing, and the dashing reputation he'd developed as a driver, had also succeeded in bringing much-needed wealth into Montacroix, a country that Burke would be the first to admit was part high-class tourist resort, part anachronism.

Indeed, a reporter for the *International Herald Tribune* had written that Montacroix had become the premier vacation destination for people whose idea of a second car was a Bentley.

The wide tires hugged the slick pavement. Burke could hardly hear himself think over the roar of the enormous rear-mounted engine situated millimeters from the back of his helmet.

After the coronation, he would probably give up this

sport he'd come to love. After all, it was one thing for an heir to the throne to be perceived as a reckless, hedonistic playboy; it was quite another for the regent to be cast in that same light.

Once he ascended to the throne, his life would inexorably change. Since duty had been drilled into him from the cradle, Burke would never think to resent what he could not change. But damn, how he wanted to go out a winner!

Suddenly, puffs of gray smoke began drifting into the cockpit. Before he had time to consider what could have gone wrong, the red Ferrari spun out of control.

Cursing, Burke twisted the steering wheel, trying to keep the race car from crashing into the storm-tossed lake.

THE RAIN CONTINUED nonstop, wrapping the palace in a soft silvery cloud that reminded Sabrina of the mists cloaking Brigadoon. After a brief, failed attempt at a nap, and a long hot bath, she'd dressed and, along with her mother and sisters, had joined the royal family for cocktails.

Chantal looked stunning, as always, in a slender tube of flame colored silk, her throat and earlobes adorned with exquisite glowing pearls. Her American husband, clad in a navy suit, was suitably handsome, providing a perfect consort for the glamorous princess, as Dixie had whispered in Sabrina's ear.

If Chantal was fire, her younger sister, the princess Noel—dressed in a silvery blue cocktail dress, her pale blond hair twisted into a tidy chignon at the nape of her slender neck—was ice. But the genuine welcome in her greeting and the warmth in her violet blue eyes belied her cool appearance.

Jessica Giraudeau, Prince Eduard's wife, was also a

shining example of warm hospitality. A superb hostess, she surprised each of her guests by revealing her knowledge of some special achievement. A former actress herself, she also made Ariel promise to tell her all the changes that had occurred in Hollywood since she'd willingly turned her back on a very successful film career for the man she loved.

Prince Eduard, too, greeted them with enthusiasm, but Sabrina could tell that he was distracted. Although he pretended to follow the polite conversation, his gaze kept drifting first to the rain-streaked windows. Then the door.

Watching him out of the corner of her eye, Sabrina could guess what had him so out of sorts. Or, more to the point, *who*. The object of his ill-concealed irritation was obviously the missing member of the Giraudeau family. The playboy prince himself.

Finally, in an attempt to maintain a facade, the little group moved to the dining room.

The vast room, which Sabrina decided could probably seat the entire New York Giants football team, was terribly overdecorated. Like much of the house it was a monument to unbridled opulence. The high ceiling was gilded, frescoes covered the walls, baroque riches filled every niche. The candlesticks on the French-lace-draped table were of Venetian rock crystal. A rare Aubusson carpet covered the floor.

Porcelain vases held more roses from the garden, orchids from the greenhouses. The chairs were gilt and appropriately spindly, save for one high-backed one at the end of the massive table that appeared more throne than chair.

"I think I know what it would feel like to dine inside a Fabergé egg," Sabrina murmured after the butler had silently whisked away their soup bowls and placed their salad plates in front of them.

Chantal, seated to Sabrina's right, glanced around the vast room as if seeing it for the first time. "*Maman* has been trying to redecorate this house since she and my father married. Unfortunately since there are a great many rooms in the palace and my father detests change, things have moved a bit more slowly than she would have liked."

"I've never seen a room like this one," Sabrina said. "Outside a museum."

"Most visitors are initially shocked by the grandeur," Chantal allowed. "In fact, the first time Caine saw it, I was afraid he'd retract his proposal and take the next plane back to Washington, alone.

"Fortunately, he resisted the impulse," she said, smiling at her husband who was seated across the table and currently involved in conversation with Raven. "Although, as you'll soon realize," Chantal said, "we live quite informally."

That may be, Sabrina considered silently, but the fact remained that this dining room alone could inspire a year's worth of sermons on conspicuous consumption.

The meal was, unsurprisingly, superb. The glazed partridge was so tender it fell off the bone, the potatoes were seasoned with fresh parsley and dressed in melted butter. Conversation flowed easily, but as the evening progressed, Sabrina noticed that Prince Eduard was glaring more and more often at the empty chair beside her.

As if conjured up by the regent's dark thoughts, Burke suddenly appeared in the dining room doorway. His face was streaked with oil, he was drenched from the rain, and a faint aroma of smoke entered the room with him.

"Good evening."

"You are late," Prince Eduard ground out with the air of a man unaccustomed to having his instructions challenged. "We are about to have dessert."

"I'm sorry about that," Burke said easily, ignoring his father's glower. "But there was a slight problem."

"Oh, dear." Jessica eyed him with motherly concern. "Is that smoke I smell?"

Burke shrugged. "A minor glitch with an oil line. Don't worry, *Maman*, it was not serious."

The fact that Jessica failed to introduce the prince to the Darlings revealed exactly how deep her concern went. "I always worry when you're in that car."

"I raced cars when you and I met," Eduard reminded his wife.

"True. But having a beau who races is a great deal different from having a son who takes unnecessary risks," Jessica pointed out.

Sabrina remembered that Burke was actually Jessica's stepson. Prince Eduard had been married—to an unstable woman who'd been hospitalized for a lifetime of mental problems—when he and the American actress first met. Their very public love affair had scandalized Europe for five years—the time it took the prince to get a divorce. That same illicit love affair had also resulted in the birth of Chantal, Sabrina remembered.

Burke crossed the priceless carpet, apparently mindless of the water sluicing off him. "I promise not to take any unnecessary risks," he said, brushing his lips against his mother's cheek. The light kiss left a smudge of oil.

After Jessica belatedly remembered her manners and introduced her son to their guests, Burke treated the women to a bold, yet repentant smile.

"I do apologize for not arriving on time to greet you all properly," he said. "But if you will forgive me, I shall excuse myself to wash the road dirt away."

His gaze, as it circled the room, treating each of the Darling women in turn to its warmth, lingered momentarily on Sabrina.

All the Darling women were surprisingly attractive, Burke conceded. Including the mother. But this one was absolutely stunning.

Her face was a classical oval, her complexion a flawless roses and cream. Her hair was a sleek flow of gold that reminded him of winter wheat warmed by a benevolent sun. Her eyes were a muted gray, touched with silver facets that glowed like moonbeams. They were fringed with a thick row of lashes and tilted up the slightest bit at the corners.

Her mouth was so full and shapely that Burke wondered if those rosy lips would be as soft as they looked. He suspected they would. The woman's only flaw was a stubborn chin, Burke decided.

As he continued to study her, color tinged her high cheekbones.

She was wearing an off-the-shoulder silky gown of hues ranging from scintillating pink to sinfully scarlet. Sparkling gold gypsy hoops hung almost to her smooth bare shoulders.

Most women Burke knew—with the exception of Chantal, who gave a new definition to the word glamour—were cut from the same expensive cloth. Sleek, rich, intelligent, and coolly sophisticated, they were women perfectly at home in European drawing rooms smelling of hothouse flowers, furniture oil and expensive, custom-blended perfumes. If they'd been cars, they would have ranked among Rolls-Royces. Or Bentleys.

This woman was more like a Ferrari. And she was not at all what he'd been expecting. So much for the cheap rhinestones and stiff cotton-candy hair, he mused, realizing that he'd been guilty of stereotyping the Darling sisters.

While Burke was studying Sabrina, she in turn was examining him. The prince had a lean, intelligent face, with good bones and nicely chiseled features, she admitted reluctantly.

Disapproving of the man's sybaritic life-style, she hadn't expected to admire anything about him. He had thick dark hair with warm sun streaks—visible proof that he didn't spend all his time inside the family palace. Sabrina had always liked brown eyes, and Prince Burke's velvet eyes were the rich hue of chocolate. And they looked as if they never missed a thing. His gaze was dark, direct, disturbing. It was hot enough to turn water to steam.

She found it difficult to think straight when he was looking at her so intently; Sabrina couldn't remember ever being so nervous. Not even seven years ago, when she'd walked onto that Broadway stage for the first time to star in her new husband's play, *Take Three.*

The blatantly autobiographical play had depicted their courtship and subsequent marriage. Unsurprisingly, given her husband's Broadway track record, it had instantly become a smash hit.

Reminding herself that she'd given up on waiting for Prince Charming to show up a very long time ago, Sabrina forced her muscles to relax.

"Burke, dear," Jessica said, her smooth silky voice finally, blessedly, shattering the expanded moment, "I believe you were about to go upstairs to change?"

"Of course."

He was speaking to his stepmother, but his eyes did

not leave Sabrina's. Something stirred inside him. *Desire*. Burke recognized it, then chose to ignore it. For now.

"I shall return shortly."

As she watched him leave the dining room, Sabrina could not decide whether to take Prince Burke's words as a promise. Or a threat.

3

THE WHITE-GLOVED BUTLER had already served dessert—sweet strawberries in champagne—when Burke returned to the dining room. He was wearing a charcoal gray Italian suit, white shirt and a red silk tie imprinted with the Giraudeau crest—a crowned lion, which thanks to Dixie's omnipresent tour book, Sabrina knew stood for the family motto *honneur, fidélité, et courage*—honor, loyalty, and bravery. His hair, still damp from his shower, was combed straight back.

After expressing his apologies once again, he sat in the empty chair next to Sabrina's. The crisp scent of pine soap clung enticingly to his tanned skin. Sabrina was vaguely surprised; she would have expected a prince to smell of some expensive, overpowering French male cologne. Her husband's cologne had given her sinus headaches, but when she'd asked him to forego the musky scent, he'd refused, instructing her to take an aspirin.

"This problem you had with the car," Prince Eduard addressed his son on a rumbling voice, "will it cause you to forfeit the race?"

Burke grinned as he put his snowy white damask napkin onto his lap. "Sorry. But it was simply a loose hose."

"Your mother worries about you." Eduard glared from beneath shaggy pewter brows, looking fierce enough to send enemies to dungeons, dangerous enough to conquer countries. But from the furrowed lines creasing the older man's forehead, Sabrina got the impression that it wasn't just Burke's mother who worried.

"I know." Burke exchanged another fond glance with Jessica. "And I promise that I will not take any undue chances."

On the other side of Sabrina, Chantal rolled her eyes and muttered something into her water goblet.

"I suppose that's all a mother can ask," Jessica agreed. Her warm gaze was laced with both acceptance and maternal concern. "However, I can't help wishing that you harbored a burning desire to be European backgammon champion, instead."

The rich deep sound of Burke's laugh plucked a distant chord within Sabrina. She frowned and directed her attention toward her dessert.

The conversation turned first toward Burke's chances of winning the Montacroix Grand Prix, and then to the upcoming coronation, and finally, Jessica amused the group by sharing stories of moviemaking during what had become known as Hollywood's golden age.

"I just realized where I've seen you before," Burke said quietly to Sabrina as his mother cheerfully described how she'd been perched atop a rock on the island of Mykonos, playing the role of a mermaid caught in a Greek fisherman's net, when she'd met the man who would become her husband.

The moment he set eyes on her, Burke had been struck by a feeling that they'd met before. He'd flipped through his mental file of names and faces while he'd showered and dressed, unreasonably frustrated when the answer hadn't come immediately to mind.

Sabrina glanced up at him, mentally bracing herself

to deny those horrid tabloid stories. She'd not have thought a prince would stoop to reading such garbage, but there had been a time when she hadn't believed that sleazy papers could get away with printing out-and-out lies, either.

During the past year, her admittedly messy divorce following her collapse onstage and her subsequent emergency surgery, and then the tragedy of her father's death had made headlines all over the world. There had been occasions when Sabrina felt as if the Darling family were keeping all those gossipy tabloids in business single-handedly.

"Oh?" she asked with blatant disinterest.

Her gaze was strangely shuttered. Burke watched the wall going up in front of him and wondered at its cause. "I was in Great Britain attending a banking summit when you performed *Private Performances* in London's West End."

The mention of that particular performance, which critics had proclaimed her best, brought back unhappy memories that Sabrina would have just as soon not discussed.

After graduation from Tennessee State College with a degree in drama, ignoring Sonny's warnings about working with damn Yankees, she'd headed north to seek her fortune on the New York stage.

Once in Manhattan, she'd quickly discovered that Sonny's name, legendary in the music business, opened no doors on Broadway. On the contrary, once she heard a director refer to her as "that little barefoot hillbilly."

Miles away from her family, homesick, discouraged and horribly lonely, Sabrina had allowed herself to be rescued yet again. This time by Arthur Longstreet, a renowned, twice-married playwright—old enough to be her father—who cast her in the lead role of his new play, made her his third wife and spent the next six years putting every aspect of their personal life up on the New York stage.

Sabrina had resented having her every thought, word and deed dissected in public. But when she professed her feelings, even that became the basis for a new story, entitled *Private Performances*.

The play, which debuted with a two-week run in Great Britain, prior to returning to Broadway's famed Majestic Theater, had been her least favorite of the six plays in which Sabrina had starred. It had also been her last.

The day she walked out on her marriage, Arthur's latest protégée—Sabrina's former understudy—took her place onstage as well as in Sabrina's bed.

"*Private Performances* sold out in four hours," Sabrina said. It had, she recalled, set a record for West End ticket sales.

"The telephone lines were jammed, making it nearly impossible to reach the box office," Burke agreed. "By the time my secretary was able to get through, all the tickets had been sold. Fortunately Diana invited me to share her box."

He mentioned the glamorous British princess with a friendly ease that led Sabrina to decide that he was not trying to impress her by name-dropping. Still, for some reason, his words rankled.

"Obviously it's true what they say—rank does have its privileges."

"Not always." Burke thought of the large, silent man who'd spent the afternoon hovering about like some overprotective guard dog. Even now the bodyguard was posted just outside the dining room door. Putting aside his frustration, Burke flashed Sabrina his practiced smile. His teeth were strong and straight and brilliantly white in his rugged, outdoors complexion.

"The two hours I spent in that darkened theater will go down as one of the highlights of my life. You were magnificent."

She'd seen that smile before, on numerous magazine covers since the announcement of Prince Burke's upcoming coronation. But no photograph had done it justice or prepared Sabrina for the effect it would have on her.

The murmur of voices, the discreet sounds of silver on china and crystal faded into the distance.

"Thank you."

"Diana and I went backstage, after the performance, to congratulate you on such a tour de force after the final curtain. But your husband informed us that you were tired and overwrought from your performance and preferred to rest."

Sabrina's temper flared. Damn Arthur! The truth was, they'd had a terrible fight before the curtain rose that night. She'd accused him of having a mistress, something he'd steadfastly denied. Right up until the end.

Obviously he'd chosen to punish her for having the nerve to question his behavior by keeping any admirers away.

No wonder her dressing room had remained depressingly empty, Sabrina realized now. At the time, she'd been devastated, believing the lack of visitors had been because the London audience hadn't enjoyed her performance.

"That night was difficult," she murmured, unwilling to admit that her former husband had wielded such iron control over her life. Control she had naively handed over when she'd married.

The day she packed her bags and left their Trump Tower apartment, Sabrina had vowed never to be that foolish again.

"And for the record, I'm never overwrought."

Burke was intrigued by the emotion that had sparked in her eyes, like the warning flash of lightning on the horizon before a thunderstorm. There was a tender spot there, he determined, choosing to ease around it, for now.

"I can certainly understand why you would have been exhausted. If anyone could have harnessed the energy you were putting out that night, they would have kept every lamp in London blazing well into the twenty-first century."

Even the usually savage British critics had raved about her performance, Burke remembered. Indeed, the normally stodgy *Times* had declared her a world-class actor, stating that the lovely young American had possessed the "Sarah Bernhardt factor."

"You're very flattering." Sabrina reluctantly gave him points for his charm.

"I'm merely stating a fact. Didn't I recently read that you were playing Maggie in *Cat on a Hot Tin Roof* in New York?"

He'd also read that she had gotten a divorce. Indeed, the so-called inside reports of her failed marriage had set new lows for an already-tawdry celebrity journalism.

Now that he'd placed her, Burke wondered why he hadn't made the connection before, when Chantal had first brought up the idea of the female trio performing for the festival. Although Sabrina had used her married name—Sabrina Longstreet—on the stage, he vaguely recalled his sister mentioning something about two of the Darling sisters being actresses.

But his mind had been on other things—the coronation, the race, and the anonymous death threats—and he hadn't really been paying attention. If he'd realized that this woman was scheduled to arrive in Montacroix, it definitely would have piqued his interest in the trio's performance.

"Actually, it was Westport, Connecticut, not Broadway. But I *was* playing Maggie. Unfortunately I had to leave in order to do the tour with my sisters."

So this singing tour wasn't her first choice. Not that he was surprised, given her acting talent. Burke wondered why a successful actress would have given up a role in which she'd received acclaim in order to suffer the rigors of life on the entertainment road.

He made a mental note to ask Chantal more about the three Darling sisters—particularly the enticing Sabrina. "I remember reading that you'd received rave reviews for that role, too." The role of Maggie suited her, Burke considered, lecturing himself for picturing her in some hot and steamy southern climate, clad only in a sexy silk slip. Even discounting her vaguely feline eyes, she radiated an almost electric sexual quality that nearly obscured the deeper vulnerability necessary for that role.

Sabrina shrugged as she took a bite of a sweet, dark red strawberry. The floaty dress slipped completely off her shoulder, revealing an intriguing bit of creamy flesh.

"Tennessee Williams wrote a powerful story. And, of course Maggie the Cat is one of those wonderful scenery-eating parts that any actress would murder for. Although I have to admit that it wasn't easy reinventing a woman from the 1950s in today's postfeminist world."

"Are you saying that Maggie couldn't exist today?"

She put down her spoon and gave Burke her full attention. "Maggie was doing her best, in her own way. She was fighting hard, with all the weapons she possessed at the time. I think that if the play were written today, that as frightening as the prospect of being alone might be, Maggie would look around and see that she had other options.

"I truly believe," she continued, "that with all her ambition and guts, she'd ultimately stop looking to her husband for her own happiness. And eventually she'd escape that cage she and Brick had somehow gotten themselves locked into."

As *she* had done. Albeit belatedly, Sabrina admitted it reluctantly. If only she'd followed her instincts and left that first year, when she had come to the unhappy realization that a handsome prince could ultimately turn out to be a frog. And a long-coveted palace could become a prison.

Burke watched the myriad of emotions come and go in her eyes. Regret, anger, determination. "Isn't it difficult to project so much raw emotion each evening?" he asked, curious as to how she managed to keep her emotional compass steady.

"Sometimes. But it's also cathartic. After all, how many people get to act out their deepest, darkest, most dangerous emotions?"

She'd never been a woman to guide her emotions, but allowed herself to be guided by them. And while she knew that many might consider such behavior foolhardy, on balance, even considering her disastrous marriage, her twenty-eight years were filled with more pleasurable memories than unhappy ones.

"And do you possess such dark and dangerous emotions?"

"Don't we all?" Her brows lifted and her chin angled slightly, as if daring him to argue.

"Touché." Since his own emotions were none too steady at the moment, Burke decided to steer the conversation back to her career. "So, is that how you choose a role? By its emotional impact on the audience?"

"Right now, I'm not exactly in the position to be choosy."

Unfortunately, as so often happens in divorces, former friends and associates had ended up taking sides. Since Arthur Longstreet's name translated into a fortune in ticket sales, and since the incestuous theater world revolved around money a great deal more than it would ever admit, Sabrina had found herself out in the cold.

"I just want to take on different and challenging parts and have the freedom to choose. Freedom," she said with a burst of feeling, "is the greatest luxury in life."

"*Rassurez-vous,* Mademoiselle Sabrina," Burke said. "I am certain that an actress of your caliber will be able to select any role you wish for as long as you continue performing."

The man was definitely smooth. No wonder he had such a reputation with the glamorous women of the Concorde Set.

"Actors come and go," she answered with the old bromide. "Only agents last forever. But I do appreciate your vote of confidence." She returned his smile with a cool, polite one of her own.

At that moment, Chantal captured everyone's attention by ringing the edge of her sterling dessert spoon against the crystal rim of her water goblet.

"I have an announcement to make." When her ver-

milion lips tilted upward in a faint, self-satisfied smile
that vaguely reminded Sabrina of the *Mona Lisa*, Caine
left his seat across the table and came to stand beside
his wife.

"You and Caine are returning to Montacroix,"
Prince Eduard guessed, crossing his arms over his
broad chest with obvious satisfaction. "It's about
time."

"Now, *Papa*," Chantal chided, "you know that
Caine's business is in Washington."

"There is more than enough work to keep your husband occupied right here," Eduard insisted gruffly.
From the resigned expressions on the faces of the other
members of the Giraudeau family, Sabrina got the impression that this was not a new argument. "Especially
now, with—"

"Why don't you let Chantal make her announcement," Burke interrupted mildly. He was smiling, but
Sabrina thought she detected a silent warning in his
dark eyes.

"A man wants his children around him when he is
entering old age," Eduard grumbled.

"You're not anywhere near approaching old age,
darling," Jessica soothed expertly. "Why, anyone can
see that you're in your prime."

"A man in his prime should have grandchildren.
Some prodigy to continue the line. Rainier has grandchildren, Philip of England has grandchildren—"

"*Papa*," Noel broke in mildly, "if you don't allow
Chantal to speak, it will be breakfast before we learn
her news."

"I was merely pointing out that you are all breaking
your mother's heart. Women need grandchildren to
spoil," Eduard insisted. "It's their nurturing nature."

"And people dare to accuse you of being a chauvinist," Noel murmured. The daughterly love in her smile took the sting out of her words. "Wherever do they get such an outlandish idea?" She turned to her sister. "Go ahead, Chantal. We're all ears."

"Actually, *Papa*, you're right." Chantal gave her father a warm and loving smile. "A man in his prime should have grandchildren."

A sudden silence descended on the room like a curtain.

"Darling," Jessica said, "are you saying—"

"Caine and I are going to have a baby." Chantal linked her beringed fingers with her husband's. When Caine lifted his wife's hand to his lips, Sabrina felt a prick of uncharacteristic envy at their obvious mutual devotion. "You, *Papa* dear, are going to be a grandfather."

For once in his life the prince was struck absolutely speechless. The entire room—Dixie, Raven, Ariel and Sabrina included—burst into delighted laughter at the sight of the stunned, red-faced patriarch.

"Well," he blustered finally, "it's high time you did your duty, Caine." He turned to the butler, who, Sabrina noticed, was grinning as widely as the rest of the family. "Joseph, this calls for champagne. Another Giraudeau is on the way!"

"Another O'Bannion," Caine corrected with a calm but steady smile.

"That, too," Eduard agreed benevolently.

After the toasts were made and the congratulations offered, Eduard turned toward his only son. "So, Burke, when are you going to follow your sister and brother-in-law's excellent example?"

Burke arched a dark brow. "You want me to father a child?"

"I want you to get married," Eduard bellowed. "Obviously the child will come after the ceremony."

"Of course," Burke murmured. "Why didn't I think of that?"

"This is no joking matter. After the coronation, your duty will no longer be to yourself, but to your country. And your first responsibility to the citizens of Montacroix is to provide the principality with an heir."

Sabrina heard Burke's slight sigh when the prince began listing suitable candidates—all, she noted, from various European nobility. It might be permissible for one of the Giraudeau princesses to marry a commoner, but obviously such independent behavior was inappropriate for the man who, in a few short days, would become regent.

"Eduard," Jessica finally broke in when the prince paused to take a breath, "we've discussed this before. You must allow our son to find his own wife. As you did," she said significantly.

"And, *grandpère*," Chantal tacked on. She turned to the Darlings, "Have you ever heard the story of our grandfather?" When Dixie stated that they hadn't, she smiled and said, "It's a wonderfully romantic story. You see, once upon a time, in a faraway kingdom called Montacroix, there was a handsome prince named Phillipe. After his graduation from Cambridge, Phillipe went to Arles on holiday. The trip was a gift from his father, Prince Léon."

"Our great-grandfather," Noel clarified.

"That's right," Chantal agreed. "Anyway, during his holiday, he happened into a cantina that featured authentic gypsy dancing."

"And it was in this cantina," Burke picked up the story, "where he first viewed the beautiful Katia, who just happened to be one of the country's most famous flamenco dancers." Burke's eyes caught Sabrina's and held for just a moment too long. "He instantly fell, as you Americans say, like a ton of bricks."

"Unfortunately," Chantal said, "Prince Léon did not feel that a foreign flamenco dancer was an appropriate wife for the future regent of Montacroix."

"But Phillipe, who had inherited the strong Giraudeau independent streak, married Katia anyway," Noel divulged. "Without great-grandfather Léon's blessing."

"Of course Léon was furious," Chantal continued.

"You see, Léon had inherited the infamous Giraudeau temper," Burke said, slanting a significant glance his father's way.

"He threatened to disinherit Phillipe," Noel said. "Which of course, he couldn't do."

"Because of the male line of ascendancy," Burke said. "Phillipe was Léon's only son. If he failed to provide a male heir, the country would return to French rule."

"But in the end, it all turned out for the best," Chantal said. "Once our father was born, great-grandfather Léon welcomed the couple back with open arms."

"So, Montacroix's future was assured, and Léon stepped down, allowing Phillipe to take his rightful place on the throne," Burke concluded.

"That's a real romantic story," Dixie said. "It sounds just like one of Sonny's ballads."

"It does, doesn't it?" Chantal agreed. "And if you think that story is romantic, you should hear how our father scandalized all of Europe when he fell madly in love with our mother."

"All right," Eduard interrupted, throwing up his hands. "I surrender. Burke, you will be permitted to select your own bride."

"Why, thank you, Father," the younger prince said with smiling formality. "That's very benevolent of you. So tell me, baby sister," he said, turning his attention to Chantal in a not-very-subtle attempt to change the subject, "what names are you and Caine considering?"

Three hours later, Sabrina was standing at the window, looking out at the star-strewed sky. You never saw stars like this in Manhattan, she mused. Nor in Nashville. Although she feared she could be guilty of romanticizing again, the sparkling pinpoints of light reminded her of diamonds scattered across lush black velvet.

Along with the starlight, a half moon slanted silvery light over the royal gardens beneath her window. In the distance, she could see the yellow glow of incandescent lights coming from some building, mute proof that she was not the only one finding sleep an elusive target.

The jet lag that had made her tired before dinner, now had her feeling wired. Her inner clock was definitely off, and Sabrina knew from experience that forcing herself to remain in bed, staring up at the ceiling while her thoughts were whirling, would only make matters worse. Eventually she'd adjust. She just had to give it time.

Worried that her continued pacing would only wake up Ariel, who was asleep in the adjoining room, Sabrina pulled on a pair of jeans and a cotton sweater and slipped out the bedroom door.

BURKE PUT AWAY the wrench, wiped his grimy hands on an equally grimy rag and grinned his satisfaction. Although he'd hired the best mechanic in Grand Prix racing, he'd always enjoyed working with engines himself.

Fortunately, as Sabrina had so succinctly stated earlier, rank did indeed have its privileges. And if the Prince of Montacroix chose to tinker with his car's engine, who was going to stop him? Of course it helped that he was very, very good at what he did.

Burke's mechanical skills were a great deal like his lovemaking talents. He took his time, absolutely refused to rush, and paid extraordinary attention to detail. The satisfaction he felt when he listened to the throaty purr of a well-tuned Ferrari engine was the same pleasure he received when he brought a woman to an earth-shattering orgasm.

He glanced down at his watch, surprised to find that it was past midnight. It had happened again; he always lost track of time when working.

"It's late," he said to the other man in the room. "You should go to bed."

Drew Tremayne, a tall muscular man who'd proved surprisingly helpful in reprogramming the computer that adjusted the fuel lines, wiped his own hands. "My replacement isn't due to show up for another hour."

"This around-the-clock surveillance is ridiculous," Burke complained.

Massive shoulders, clad in a black fisherman's sweater designed to blend into the night shadows, lifted, then dropped again. "Caine likes to cover all the bases. That's why he's so good."

A perfectionist himself, Burke could appreciate such a trait in others. He knew Caine was intelligent, incisive and every bit as single-minded as Burke himself was.

During the two years the former naval aviator and presidential security agent had been married to his sis-

ter, Burke had come to know his brother-in-law well.
Caine was not a man with doubts. He was also not a
man to overestimate danger. If he felt that these recent
threats were legitimate, if he believed the rebels intended to attempt to disrupt the coronation, Burke had
no choice but to believe him.

That didn't mean, however, that he had to like it.

"From what he says, you're not so bad, yourself," he
said.

The harsh mouth, which Burke had thus far only
seen set in a grim straight line, curved upward in a
bold grin, revealing a chipped front tooth that gave
him a vaguely wolfish look.

"He's got to say that," Drew said on a slow drawl
that attested to seven generations of Tennessee ancestors. "I'm his partner."

"Which says a lot right there. Caine would never settle for second best." Which was the reason he'd married Chantal, Burke considered.

"Caine and I have had some high old times together," Drew agreed, with what Burke suspected was
typical understatement. He pulled a chocolate bar out
of his pocket, unwrapped it, and offered a piece to
Burke, who refused.

Drew was a nice man. Still, Burke realized that his
bodyguard's easygoing exterior was camouflage for a
quick mind and, if necessary, a willingness to indulge
in violence. Burke knew from the way this man handled his Beretta, that he could not be in better hands.

Still, the idea of even needing a bodyguard continued to sting. Frowning at the idea of having a shadow
for the next nine days, Burke glanced idly out the open
garage door. When he caught a glimpse of pale blond
hair shimmering in the moonlight, he cursed.

"I thought my sisters had been assigned bodyguards as well."

"They have."

"Then what the hell is Noel doing out wandering out in the garden alone?"

Drew's puzzled frown was even darker than Burke's. He pulled the pistol from its leather holster at the back of his belt. "Wait here."

"She's my sister," Burke complained. "If she's in danger, I want to help her."

"Fine. So help her by not screwing things up."

Frustrated, but realizing this mountain of a man had a point—after all, his experience with guns was limited to shooting clay pigeons on the palace gunnery range—Burke reluctantly agreed. He ground his teeth as he watched Drew slip out of the garage, blending into the dark shadows.

After what seemed an eternity, but was only moments, Drew returned, emerging from the dark with the same unnerving skill he'd used to disappear.

"It's not the princess," he answered Burke's sharp, questioning glance. "It's one of those singers. Sabrina Darling."

That explained the blond hair he'd mistaken for Noel's. "Did she see you?"

"Nah. I didn't want to scare her. I was tempted to ask for her autograph, though," Drew admitted sheepishly.

"You've seen her act?"

"No, I can't say I've ever had the privilege. But I sure do remember when she was on TV with her daddy. I've always been a big Sonny Darling fan," he revealed on a slow drawl that belied his quick mind. "Saw him once in concert, back home in Tennessee. That man sure could hold an audience."

"Obviously, at least one of his daughters inherited that talent," Burke said, remembering how she'd held him spellbound for two amazing hours in that London theater.

"They're all good," Drew allowed. "Although it was a long time ago, and I was just a kid, I can remember critics saying that of the three Little Darlings, Ariel had the beauty and Raven had the voice. But Sabrina had inherited her daddy's ability to sell a song."

Burke believed it. From what he'd seen of Sabrina thus far, he decided that she was a woman who could probably sell antifreeze to the Arabs.

An unpalatable thought suddenly occurred to him. "If we thought she was Noel—"

"There's a good chance someone else might make the same mistake," Drew cut in. "Which is why I radioed for one of the guys inside the palace to come outside and keep an eye on her."

"That's very efficient," Burke allowed.

"You get what you pay for."

"Still, it'd probably be better if Ms. Darling was inside, where she belonged."

"True enough," Drew agreed. "But I decided hogtying her and dragging her back to her bedroom might be overkill."

Burke smiled at that provocative image. If he had to be stuck with a bodyguard, Burke decided he could have done a lot worse than this friendly giant.

"Why don't I give it a try?" he suggested.

"Good idea," Drew said as he opened a bag of chocolate-covered peanuts. "I imagine there's not many women who could resist a true-to-life prince."

Since the easily stated remark was reasonably true, Burke did not comment on it. "It's no wonder you and Chantal get along so well," Burke observed, casting a disparaging glance at the bright yellow candy bag. "Between the two of you, you must keep the world's chocolatiers in business."

"That's pretty much what Caine says," Drew agreed equably. "But then, your brother-in-law is one of those health nuts who gets up in the morning and wolfs down a bowl of nuts and twigs. Lord, I used to hate doin' stakeouts with that man."

Burke laughed, swallowed the last of the too sweet coffee Drew had poured them earlier from an insulated metal thermos, and left the garage.

The lone figure silhouetted in the upstairs palace window, observing the woman walking in the garden, also witnessed the bodyguard's cloaked surveillance.

Now, alone and shrouded by darkness, the figure watched intently as Prince Burke approached Sabrina Darling.

Was this midnight rendezvous merely coincidence? the silent observer wondered. Or was it preplanned? A romantic tryst, perhaps?

The answer, the interested onlooker mused thoughtfully, might prove very interesting indeed.

4

SABRINA WANDERED through the royal garden maze, inhaling the sweet perfume that wafted on the still night air. Having grown accustomed to the night sounds of Manhattan—the traffic, the sirens, the blare of horns of the *New York Times* trucks racing down Broadway—she found the silence immensely soothing. It reminded her of lazy summer nights on her family's Nashville farm.

But Montacroix was a long, long way from Nashville. And although the house that Sonny Darling's royalties had built had once seemed the most magnificent home in the world, she now realized that as impressive as it had been, it was not the dazzling white palace she once believed it to be.

She shook her head, remembering how she'd believed her father to be a fairy-tale prince, come to carry her off to his castle, where she'd live happily ever after.

She'd been so young. So naive.

"So stupid," Sabrina muttered now. Experience had taught her the hard way that any woman foolish enough to believe in happily-ever-afters was destined to be disappointed.

"Excuse me." Startled by Burke's unexpected appearance, Sabrina jumped as he emerged from the shadows. "I did not mean to intrude on your privacy."

If there was one thing six years of marriage had taught her, it was to recognize a prevarication when she heard one. Some inner voice told her that Burke was lying.

"It appears that I was about to intrude on yours," she said, regaining her composure. She glanced past him at the now-dark building. "How's the car coming?"

The scent of gardenias rose from her skin, blending with the sweet perfume of the roses on the summer air. Her eyes, in the slanting moonlight, were the hue of sterling buffed to a warm sheen.

"There was an additional problem with the fuel mixture—the engine was running too lean—but I believe the situation is solved."

"Did you check the microchips in the fuel computer?"

Burke gave her a sharp look that revealed his surprise. "The crew had installed the wrong chips. How did you guess?"

"My father was a die-hard racing fan. He drove stock cars when he was younger, but by the time I came along, Dixie had put her foot down about his racing and he had to console himself with just being a spectator. But he never lost his love of cars. When I was sixteen, when one of his albums went platinum, he bought a bright red Ferrari. A convertible, like Magnum P.I. drove."

"Ferraris are very fine automobiles." Burke had a Testarossa, along with a white winged Lamborghini Countach and Mercedes roadster parked in the palace garage.

"It was certainly a very fast car. Unfortunately fast cars have always been my secret weakness."

She hadn't owned a car in Manhattan; Arthur didn't drive and refused to pay for garage space for the sporty Mustang convertible she'd left at the farm in Nashville.

Once again Burke saw the flash of annoyance come and go in her eyes. Once again he wondered at its cause.

"Daddy emphatically declared it off-limits, but I couldn't resist and one night, when he was away on tour, I borrowed it."

Forgetting that it was unwise to relax her guard around this man, Sabrina sighed with reminiscent pleasure. "I had it up to one hundred and ten miles an hour before the highway patrol caught me in a speed trap."

"You could have been killed." He could see her, racing down the highway, her hair streaming out behind her like a silver banner.

"That's what Daddy said. But he put it a bit more strongly." Her remarkable eyes were still laughing. "In fact, his language could have stripped paint. I was grounded for six months, but he gave in and suspended sentence after two weeks."

Burke wasn't surprised by her father's surrender. He had a feeling it would be very difficult to deny this woman anything.

"That doesn't explain how you knew about the fuel chips."

"Oh, that. My father took the entire family to the Indianapolis 500 every year. And when he performed in Arizona, I flew out to see him and we went to the Phoenix Grand Prix. It was the most exciting thing I've ever seen.

"Dad had a pit pass," Sabrina said offhandedly, as if such extraordinary privilege were run-of-the-mill. "I remember one of the drivers having a problem with his engine. It turned out to be the microchips."

She had bittersweet memories of that halcyon afternoon. It was the last time she'd seen her father alive. If she'd only known, Sabrina considered, she would have cherished the day even more.

Burke viewed the shutter that seemed to come down over her eyes and heard her faint sigh. "I'm sorry about your loss," he murmured. "It always hurts to lose family."

After six months, the loss of her father still stung. Sabrina suspected it would for a very long time. Yet, after all the many words of condolences she'd received, Burke's simple statement touched her.

She didn't know that his own mother had been institutionalized when he was a mere infant. Yet when he'd learned that Clea Giraudeau had died by her own hand, three years ago, Burke had experienced a deep, visceral sense of loss.

"It was so sudden," she murmured, as much to herself as to him. "And so unexpected."

She felt the sting of hot tears burning at the back of her lids and blinked them away. "Daddy always seemed larger than life. And although I know that it's irrational, I believed he'd always be there for me. For all of us."

However, Sonny Darling had, unfortunately, proved distressingly human.

"I've often felt the same way about my own father," Burke allowed. "Some men—some people—seem invincible. Although I've spent a lifetime preparing to be regent, lately I've worried about living up to the high standards set by my father."

Burke was shocked to hear himself admit such a personal thought to a virtual stranger.

Sabrina Darling affected more than his hormones. She was, surprisingly, distracting his mind.

"From everything Chantal has told me, I have no doubt that you'll be a wonderful ruler."

Burke searched her face, seeking some flaw, some imperfection that would deflate the wild, romantic fantasies that had sprung full-blown in his mind.

Her lips lured; her scent enticed. His mouth was so very close to hers. All he'd have to do is lean forward, the least little bit and...

A gust of wind blew in off the lake, causing the nighttime temperature to suddenly drop. Sabrina shivered.

The involuntary shudder didn't escape Burke's shrewd eyes.

"You should go back inside," he suggested, remembering his reason for seeking her out in the first place. "Before you catch a cold."

"I suppose I should." Her heart was thumping uncomfortably. What was it about this man that made her throat dry up and her nerves jangle?

Burke watched her lips tighten and mistook the reason for her frown. "I'm sorry if I saddened you by bringing up memories of your father."

"It wasn't you." With a wistful sigh, she looked out over the moon-gilded waters of the lake. "I think about him all the time."

"It sounds as if you and he were very close."

"I adored him," Sabrina said simply.

A very strong part of Sabrina still did. Another part which she knew to be irrational, continued to be angry at her father for not having been perfect.

"Enough to put aside your career to pay his tax bills?" It was a shot in the dark, gleaned from something Chantal had told him after dinner. If his sister had found his sudden interest in Sabrina strange, she had been thoughtful enough not to comment.

"My father was not a tax dodger!" Sabrina rose quickly and heatedly to Sonny's defense. Just because she was angry with him didn't mean that her loyalty toward the man had diminished.

"I'm sorry. I did not mean to offend you. Or your late father."

Sabrina knew that her quick flare of anger had been an inappropriate response. She'd always had difficulty controlling the Darling temper, especially when her nerves were on edge.

"No, I'm the one who should apologize for snapping at you. Especially since it's true that the only reason we're on tour is to try to pay off the IRS." Indeed, they'd signed an agreement that all royalties earned on album sales went directly to the government.

Burke had always admired family loyalty. "Repaying your father's debt is an admirable undertaking."

Sabrina made a vague gesture. "It's not at all admirable. It's simply necessary. And although I'll admit to being a little touchy about the subject, that still didn't give me an excuse to bite your head off."

She managed a faint, self-deprecating smile. "I don't suppose I could get away with blaming it on jet lag?"

Burke didn't immediately answer. A brief silence settled over them. He found Sabrina as intriguing as she was finding him unsettling.

Having grown up with two half sisters, Burke knew that the clever use of cosmetics could make a pretty woman beautiful and a beautiful woman stunning. But Sabrina Darling was one of those rarest of women, a true natural beauty.

In heavy stage makeup, she appeared lush and sultry and vampish; at dinner, she'd possessed a nonconformist, individualistic type of glamour. But in the moonlight, with her bare face revealing a dusting of freckles, Sabrina Darling seemed delicate and vulnerable.

"A woman as lovely as you could use any excuse and a man would have no choice but to forgive her."

His voice was smooth and silky. Something in his gaze set off warning bells.

"Is that a pass, Your Highness?" she managed with far more aplomb than she was feeling.

"Not a pass, merely the truth," Burke assured her mildly. "I'm sure your presence—and that of your lovely sisters, of course—shall add much to the up-coming celebrations," he added, swiftly changing the direction of the conversation.

Still vaguely shaken by the flare of desire she'd witnessed in his midnight dark eyes, Sabrina gave him a distant smile.

"You're right. I really should be going in," she said. "I've got a busy day tomorrow. Today," she amended. "We need to check out the theater, begin interviewing musicians and, of course, we'll have to coordinate logistics with the coronation committee."

"I will personally ask the members of the committee to help you in every way. Will using local talent be a problem?"

Sabrina shrugged. "Nothing we can't deal with." She neglected to mention that Raven had hit the roof when informed that they wouldn't be able to bring along their own keyboard player, drummer and guitarists.

"I realize that the situation is not ideal," Burke allowed. "But when the opposition objected to having a foreign group perform, I felt that a compromise was in order."

"Opposition?" Sabrina gave him a sharp, probing glance. "Please tell me that we're not going to get booed when we come out onstage." *Wouldn't that make terrific press.*

"You needn't worry. The malcontents are a very small group. Unfortunately they tend to also be very vocal, but I assure you that I won't allow them to disrupt either the ceremony or your performance." His tone provided immediate reassurance.

"It must be nice, having your own country." *And making your own laws.* The subtle accusation, unspoken, hovered between them on the perfumed night air.

"It has its moments," Burke agreed amiably.

Her extraordinary eyes, her soft, throaty voice, pulled him in two contradictory directions. Move closer. Back away. The second option was safer, the first eminently more appealing.

"Let me escort you back to the house." He slipped his hands into the pockets of his jeans, resisting a sudden impulse to run his fingers through the golden slide of her hair.

Quicksand, Burke warned himself. Take one more step and you're lost. For some reason that he didn't want to dwell on, the idea was inordinately tempting.

As they walked back to the palace, side by side, Burke was all too aware of the ever-present shadow trailing a discreet distance behind.

Burke was almost grateful for Drew Tremayne's silent presence. It had been one more reason for not giving in to temptation and kissing Sabrina Darling in the moonlight.

And as attractive as he admittedly found her, she was a complication he honestly didn't need. Not now. Not with everything else that was happening in his life.

Sabrina was surprised when the tall double doors, which Dixie had informed them originally belonged to an ancient monastery, swung open at their arrival. The servant, a tall muscular young man in his early thirties, greeted Sabrina and the prince with a polite nod of his prematurely gray head.

"Do the servants always stay up until the entire family is in bed?" she asked as she and Burke climbed the ornate curving stairway to the family quarters.

"Kirk is very loyal," Burke answered obliquely, unprepared to let Sabrina in on the small fact that Kirk Peterson was a former U.S. government agent, now in the employ of O'Bannion and Tremayne Security, Inc.

"He must be," Sabrina murmured. "To still be up at this hour."

She wondered idly what it would be like to have so many people at your beck and call, and decided it would be suffocating. Sabrina found herself almost feeling sorry for Burke. They'd reached the door to her family's suite. They stood there, face-to-face, for a long, silent time, both loath to leave, and both equally reluctant to admit it.

"If you'd like, it would be my pleasure to give you the grand tour of the royal theater tomorrow." Burke kept his voice low, to keep from disturbing her mother and sisters.

"Thanks, but as I told you, we've got a lot to do. And Noel's already arranged to show us the ropes."

"If you need any help locating musicians—"

"Chantal's taken care of it. The first audition is scheduled for eight-thirty."

"So soon," Burke murmured, glancing down at his watch. Her schedule certainly didn't allow for much sleep.

"There's a great deal to do. And not much time in which to do it," she said. Her own voice was little more than a whisper but easily heard in the hushed stillness of the palace hallway. "We want everything to be perfect."

So, she, too, was a perfectionist. Burke told himself that along with an intense loyalty to family, this was another thing they had in common. Not that he was keeping score, he assured himself quickly.

"Well, then, I'll say good night." He took her hand, as if to give it a polite handshake.

"Yes." As his long dark fingers curled warmly around hers, Sabrina's feet seemed nailed to the floor. A trickle of anticipation raced along her skin. Even as common sense told her she should pull her hand away, Sabrina allowed it to linger in his much larger one, pleasing them both. "Good night, Your Highness."

Caprice was an alien concept to Burke. Giving in to a rare impulse, he lifted her crimson tipped fingers to his lips.

"*Bonne nuit, Mademoiselle Sabrina.*"

Burke's rich, deep voice, the touch of his lips against her skin, the warmth of his gaze, all conspired to stir something elemental inside her.

Oh, no, Sabrina begged silently. *Please. Not again.*

It wouldn't happen.

She wouldn't let it happen.

Even as she vowed not to make the mistake of falling in love with a man who was admittedly a dead ringer for that Prince Charming who'd starred in so many youthful romantic fantasies, Sabrina was still dwelling on that warm, wonderful, stimulating feeling twenty minutes later, as she finally drifted off to sleep in the magnificent canopied bed.

THE ROYAL MONTACROIX theater seemed, at first glance, to be a marzipan building decked with paper flags. A towering structure that seemed to belong more to fantasy than reality, on the outside, it was a dazzling alabaster affair of wedding-cake spires and cupolas trimmed in rich, gleaming gold.

Inside there were ascending rows of rich red velvet chairs, an Ionic colonnade trimmed with marble theatrical masks and garlands, and a trompe l'oeil coffered ceiling, adorned with the same gilt that dazzled the eye on the exterior of the building. Between the Ionic pillars were towering mirrors, designed to reflect the movement onstage, surrounding the audience with dramatic action.

Behind the scenes, the stage machinery consisted of an ancient yet still operating system of thick, hand-hewn beams and elaborately designed contraptions of block and tackle and cables. Fortunately, Sabrina discovered over the next three days of rehearsal, the architect of this fairy-tale theater had been ahead of his time when it came to acoustics—they were remarkable. And the lighting, while far from state of the art, was more than adequate for their purposes. The one glitch was the need for additional power to run the computerized video equipment.

Following the lead of Natalie Cole, who'd achieved unprecedented success by singing duets with old televised performances of her father, Dixie had come up with the idea of Sonny Darling's three daughters singing along with him, in the same way they had when they were girls.

Although the idea of having the Darling sisters perform in Montacroix had been Chantal's idea, Sabrina quickly noticed that it was Noel who provided the upcoming concert's adept organizational skills. She was a paragon of quiet efficiency.

On the afternoon of her fourth day in the principality, Sabrina was in the theater, rehearsing with her sisters and the musicians when the lights flickered overhead and went out. The enormous screen darkened; Sonny's larger-than-life picture faded from view. "We've obviously overloaded the electrical system," Raven decided, her voice echoing in the empty, cavernous, turn-of-the-century theater.

"I'd say that's a distinct possibility," Noel, who'd been watching from the wings, agreed. She picked up the cellular phone she seemed never to be without and made the call to the director of palace maintenance. "An electrician will arrive momentarily."

"It's just as well the power went out," Ariel decided. "My throat's a little scratchy. I think I'd better have some tea."

"With honey and lemon," Noel said knowingly. "I've a thermos right here."

Having watched her in action for the past three days, Sabrina was not surprised that Noel not only knew of Ariel's preferred throat-soothing drink, but also had it on hand.

"I think I'll take a walk while we wait for the power to come back on," Sabrina said. "All the coffee I've had this morning has left me a little edgy."

She was not about to admit that it had been too many sleepless nights that had her nerves on edge— nights spent gazing out her window toward the lighted garage and picturing Burke hunkered over his beloved race car.

She hadn't seen him since their conversation in the gardens. He'd not shown up for breakfast or dinner, and during the day, she had immersed herself in rehearsals, while Burke was occupied with time trials and the whirl of social events that were part of every Grand Prix event.

Sabrina told herself that she should not care what

Burke was doing. She assured herself that she had absolutely no interest in the playboy prince.

So why, she had asked herself innumerable times during the past three days, did her mind continually drift toward Prince Burke? And why had she found the picture of him in this morning's paper, with Monaco's glamorous Princess Caroline, so disturbing?

Sabrina had never experienced such a surge of hot, feminine jealousy as that caused by the sight of Burke's devastating smile directed the princess's way. Not even on that fateful day when she'd returned home early from the doctor and discovered her husband in bed with his mistress.

She left the stage and was halfway down the center aisle, headed toward the towering doors at the back of the theater, when a lone figure rose from one of the lush red chairs on the aisle.

"Oh!" The exclamation escaped her lips on a quick, surprised rush of breath.

"I seem to have an unfortunate knack of startling you," Burke said as his gaze skimmed over her.

The first time he'd seen Sabrina Darling, she'd reminded him of a gypsy. Today she was wearing a black-and-white striped T-shirt, short black skirt, and black beret tilted over her blond hair that brought to mind an Apache dancer.

"I hope you don't think I have a habit of lurking in the darkness like a phantom to frighten women, Mademoiselle Sabrina."

"Of course not, Your Highness." She used his title as protocol demanded. But refusing to give him the upper hand, she dispensed with the accompanying curtsy that Dixie's ubiquitous tour book had stated was appropriate behavior. "But, you did surprise me. I didn't know you were in the theater."

"I finished a qualifying run and decided to come listen to your rehearsal."

He'd found her performance spellbinding.

Sabrina waited for Burke to say something about their rehearsal. When he didn't, she forced down her disappointment and said, "How did you finish?"

Her lips were a natural dusty rose. Once again he found himself fantasizing about their taste. "Finish?"

"You said you'd just finished a qualifying run. So how did you do?"

"Oh, that." He shrugged, his mind not at all on the race. Instead he pictured making love with this woman on the teak deck of the royal yacht while the craft bobbed gently on the sparkling waters of Lake Losange. "I finished first."

His tone was matter-of-fact, but his eyes were unnervingly intimate, making Sabrina feel off balance. It was not a feeling she cared for.

"Congratulations."

"Thank you."

The formally polite conversation came to another lingering halt as they stood there, inches apart, studying each other.

Finally Sabrina couldn't take Burke's silent scrutiny another moment. She folded her arms over the front of her striped shirt and said, "Well?"

"Well?" Burke repeated.

Her palms were damp with nerves. Such weakness irritated Sabrina. Pushing an impatient hand through her thick fall of wheat blond hair, she said, "Well, will we do?"

Lord, she had beautiful hands, Burke considered.

A vision of her slim fingers with those daring red fingernails slowly unfastening the buttons of his shirt, then pressing provocatively against his bare chest flashed seductively through his mind.

Burke slid his hands into the pockets of his jeans and frowned.

Protocol and impeccable manners befitting royalty had been drilled into him by first his father, then a series of strict German nuns, and, finally, the harsh headmaster of the British boys' military academy he'd attended before reading law and banking at Oxford. His mind never wandered, even during the most excruciatingly dull conversations and never, in all his thirty-six years, had his body responded so mutinously to the mere proximity of any woman. In truth, when a man was wealthy, unattached and reasonably good-looking, women were in steady supply. That being the case, Burke had always taken members of the opposite sex somewhat for granted.

But dammit, he wanted Sabrina. He had wanted her from that first blinding moment their eyes had met across the palace dining room, and although he'd steadfastly avoided the impossibly sexy woman for three entire days, all he'd managed to do was increase his craving for her.

"You will more than *do*, mademoiselle. You and your equally lovely sisters will set the standard."

"That's very kind of you to say."

Her warm, throaty voice curled around Burke like smoke.

The absolute truth was that he was having more and more trouble remembering what they were talking about. "I am extremely grateful that you have agreed to perform for my coronation ceremonies."

Once again Sabrina felt herself succumbing to dual feelings of both discomfort and curiosity. For the first time in her life, she finally understood why that proverbial moth was drawn to the deadly flame of the funeral pyre.

"Well, we're certainly grateful for the opportunity." She brushed her hair behind her shoulder with a quick, absent flick. "And we're definitely looking forward to performing for you."

Her words amused him, although he managed to keep the humor from showing on his face. She was a liar. But such a lovely one, he couldn't resist baiting her. Just a little.

"That's not exactly what I heard." His eyebrows rose only a fraction, but enough to register his disbelief.

Sabrina felt the warm color rise in her cheeks and was grateful for the subdued lighting. "If I was at all hesitant, when Princess Chantal first requested we perform, it was because I didn't believe that our music was in keeping with the solemnity of the occasion."

Good. Her voice was cool and calm and belied her embarrassment that the prince had been told of her initial reluctance.

She had, of course, been outvoted. Both Ariel and Raven, not to mention Dixie, had jumped at what they considered a golden opportunity. Which it had turned out to be, Sabrina was forced to admit.

As soon as Mary Hart had announced the news of their upcoming Montacroix concert on *Entertainment Tonight*, the remaining three months of their nine-month tour immediately sold out. In fact, the promoter was considering adding second shows in Dallas, Los Angeles, and a third in Las Vegas.

He arched a dark brow. "You expected me to prefer Mozart? Or Bach?"

"Something along those lines." Sabrina remembered what Chantal had said about Prince Eduard's preference for chamber music.

"Mozart will be performed at the actual coronation. But the family wanted something contemporary for the public celebration."

"Chantal assured us that we were exactly what the coronation committee was looking for."

Actually, she'd said something about shaking up a few old fogies, but Sabrina decided, for the sake of discretion, not to reveal that little bit of information.

"Chantal can be quite persuasive when she puts her mind to something."

"So I've heard."

Sabrina recalled reading an interview in *Vanity Fair* where Montacroix's quintessential princess stated that she'd known right away that the dashing secret service man was destined to be her life mate. It had, Chantal had admitted blithely, taken a bit longer for Caine to accept that idea.

The door behind them opened with a blinding flash of summer sunlight that turned Sabrina's hair to molten gold. The electrician Noel had summoned entered the theater with a self-confident swagger, tool belt swung low on his hips like a gunfighter.

"Well, glory be, if it isn't the answer to all our prayers," Ariel called out on that same husky Southern voice daytime television viewers had come to know so well. It was, Sabrina thought with an inner smile, the voice of a woman interested in a man.

Since Sonny's death, Dixie had become even more vocal in her desire for a grandchild. Perhaps, Sabrina considered, Ariel might be the one to get their mother off their collective backs.

After collapsing onstage during the second act of *Private Performances*, Sabrina had undergone an emergency operation that had left her unable to ever have children. At the time, Arthur had assured her that it didn't matter. They had, after all, agreed that they didn't want children.

Afterward, when she had escaped her husband's controlling attitude and had begun to think for herself, Sabrina had realized that it had been Arthur who had never wanted a child. And, like everything else in their marriage, Sabrina, eager to please, desperate to be loved and accepted, had simply gone along.

Faced with the knowledge that she would never be a mother, Sabrina had experienced a deep sense of loss. But then she'd gotten the plum role of Maggie and was too busy with work to dwell on her loss. But there was still not a day that went by that Sabrina didn't feel a fleeting pang of regret.

"The lights will probably be back on soon," she said, thinking that the electrician would undoubtedly work at triple speed to impress her sister. Then again, he might be reluctant to rush the job, which would require him to leave. Sabrina had seen it happen before—grown men practically falling all over themselves to earn so much as a glance from Ariel Darling. Having been absolutely faithful and sheltered during her ill-fated marriage, what Sabrina had failed to see—and what her controlling husband had known too well—was that most males behaved in much the same manner around her.

"I think Bernard wants very much to impress your sister," Burke agreed, dragging his gaze from Sabrina to watch the man practically preening like a cock out to impress a hen.

"It happens all the time. Ariel's the beauty of the family," Sabrina said without rancor. "She takes after Dixie."

Burke sensed that Sabrina was genuinely unaware of being the true beauty in the Darling family. He found himself wishing that the coronation ball was tonight. It would give him an excuse to dance with her. Burke had the feeling that Sabrina Darling was the type of woman who'd fit superbly into a man's arms. And his bed.

The look he was giving her made her blood hum, her heart beat faster and her knees turn weak and rubbery. Sabrina felt as if she'd just run a marathon.

She let out a shaky breath. "Well, as much as I've enjoyed our little chat, I wanted to get some exercise in before we resume rehearsing. Your chef is so wonderful, if I don't watch out, I'll end up looking like the Pillsbury Doughboy."

"I find that highly unlikely."

"Well, since I can't afford to outgrow all those costumes Dixie bought for the next few months, I thought I'd take a walk along the lakefront."

"An excellent idea." Burke backed away, allowing her to pass. "Enjoy your stroll."

She could feel his gaze as she made her way up the aisle. She swore not to look back, but of course she did. Her eyes met his and although the sky outside the theater was a clear, alpine blue, Sabrina could have sworn she heard the clap of thunder.

Furious at herself for allowing him to get under her skin this way, she tossed her head with a flare of annoyance.

Burke nodded, accepting her unspoken challenge.

Unsure whether she was running from him or her own dangerous fantasies, Sabrina spun around and marched quickly out of the theater, slamming the enormous door behind her.

Immersed in her own nervousness, she failed to notice that the moment she left the building, she acquired a silent, shadowy escort.

Up on the stage, Ariel and Raven, who'd been watching the encounter with unabashed interest, exchanged a look. And then a smile.

"Is it me, or did the temperature in here take a sudden rise?" Ariel murmured, fanning herself dramatically with her sheet music.

Dixie, who'd been sitting in the front row, had also not missed the exchange between her stepdaughter and the prince.

"Sabrina deserves a fantasy romance," she declared. "After all that low-down snake of a husband put her through."

"Sabrina and a prince," Ariel said on a long, drawn-out sigh. "It would be like a fairy tale."

Raven, the sole pragmatist in the colorfully theatrical Darling family, looked worried. "It could also be a disaster," she warned. "Sabrina's been through a rough time, which makes her extremely vulnerable right now. And everyone knows the prince's reputation with women."

As he approached the stage, Burke couldn't help overhearing snippets of their conversation.

Having been born into the royal family, he'd lived his entire life in the glare of the international spotlight. Exaggerated reports of his exploits with the opposite sex had never disturbed him. He had, with his innately pragmatic view of life, merely considered the source.

He'd also noticed, with some amusement, that whenever he appeared on the cover of one of those gossip magazines, tourism—his country's lifeblood—increased. It was a private Giraudeau joke; there had been many times when he'd complained that although escorting the world's beauties was difficult work, he would make the sacrifice, for family and country.

He had an urge to reassure Sabrina's family that he

was not the rogue Raven, at least, perceived him to be. With a self-discipline that had always served him well, Burke resisted that urge.

As he gave his compliments to Sabrina's talented sisters, Burke kept thinking about that heated challenge he'd seen in Sabrina's silver eyes.

There had been nothing subtle about that look. Indeed, she might as well have taken a gauntlet and slapped him across the cheek.

An expert fencer, Burke had never been one to back away from a challenge. This was going to be, he decided with a slow, inward smile, a most enjoyable duel.

5

"So," ARIEL SAID that evening as they dressed for dinner, "has he kissed you yet?"

Sabrina knew better than to pretend that she didn't know what her sister was talking about. "No. And he's not going to, either. Not if I have anything to say about it."

"I don't know," Raven argued as she rolled an ebony silk stocking up one long leg, "from the way you two were lighting up the royal theater, I'd guess that you're both suffering from a lot of stored-up sexual energy."

"I haven't thought about sex since my divorce," Sabrina said, not quite truthfully.

Just last night she'd had a dream in which Burke had played a starring role. The erotically vivid dream had left her shaken. And wanting.

"Besides, I'd rather concentrate on my work." She cast a warning glance toward the adjacent bathroom, where the maid was preparing Dixie's bath.

"All work and no play..." Ariel warned. Wrapped in a thick royal blue towel, she began digging through the drawers of the antique armoire. "Has anyone seen my beaded sweater?"

"Not since Philadelphia," Sabrina answered.

"Oh, damn, I remember now. I sent it down to the concierge to be cleaned." She tapped a pink fingernail against her front tooth. "I hate life on the road."

"I don't know," Dixie drawled sapiently, stretching out on a pink satin lounge that looked as though it might have belonged to Marie Antoinette, "sometimes it has its advantages."

She popped a Swiss chocolate from a silver tray into her mouth. "This is sure a long, long way from the kind of places your daddy stayed in when he started out on the road."

"Don't get used to this," Raven warned. She stood and twisted around in order to check that the sexy seams running up her black hose were straight. "Because in six more days we'll be back in the real world."

"From the way his royal highness has been looking at Sabrina," Ariel said, her voice muffled by the white silk camisole she was pulling over her head, "I'd say that there's a good chance one of us will be staying here in Fantasyland."

"Speaking of fantasies—"

Before Sabrina could finish her retort, the young maid appeared in the doorway. "Would madame and mesdemoiselles wish anything else?"

"You've done quite enough, Monique dear," Dixie said with her trademark smile.

"More than enough," Sabrina said under her breath.

Although Monique was as polite and as efficient as Chantal had promised, the way she was always hovering nearby, eager to help, made Sabrina uncomfortable. Earlier this evening, she and Monique had gotten into a contretemps when she'd insisted on running her own bathwater.

Dixie, overhearing Sabrina's remark, gave her daughter a slightly censorious look and said, "I believe we can muddle through for the rest of the evening ourselves, Monique. But thank you so much for all you've done." Another smile, even more dazzling than the first. "No one's ever ironed the pleats on my green dress so perfectly."

"Thank you, Madame Darling." The young woman's doe brown eyes were overbrimming with gratitude. "I shall be in my room in the servant's wing. If there is anything else you need, anything at all—"

"We'll call you," Dixie agreed. "Good night, Monique."

"*Bonne nuit, madame.*" Monique backed out of the room on a subservient bow. "*Bonne nuit, mesdemoiselles.*"

"Such a sweet girl," Dixie murmured. "And so polite. Now," she said, turning back toward Sabrina, "what were you saying, darling?"

"I was saying that Ariel has obviously spent too many years in Hollywood." She frowned as she concentrated on applying a sweep of rose blush to her cheekbones. "Life," she pointed out briskly, "is not some soap opera."

"Well, I know that." Ariel deftly piled her hair into a precarious twist atop her head, securing it with a diamond clasp. "But, I gotta tell you, little sister, if any man ever looked at me the way that prince has been looking at you ever since we arrived, I'd hightail it right down to Neiman Marcus and start shopping for a trousseau."

"And you all accuse me of being the family romantic," Sabrina muttered.

"I think Ariel's got a point, baby," Dixie said, licking chocolate from her fingertips. "It's obvious that the man's downright smitten with you."

Sabrina arched an amused brow. "Smitten?" She reached for the one somber item in her wardrobe—a dress she'd bought to wear to her father's funeral.

"Honestly, Mama, if the man is interested, it's merely sex."

"Lots of long-standing marriages start out based on sex." Dixie's knowing tone gave Sabrina a surprising, intimate glimpse into her father and stepmother's relationship.

"Now we're talking about marriage?"

At the last moment, her hand, as if acting on its own volition, plucked a gold-tissue lamé slip dress from its padded satin hanger. The devastatingly sexy dress had been purchased specifically for the tour with funds Dixie had charmed from a Nashville National Trust bank vice president.

As Dixie had pointed out during a whirlwind shopping spree in Atlanta reminiscent of Sherman's march through Georgia, it was important to the success of the tour that the girls looked like the stars they were. And if that meant going even deeper into debt, then that's exactly what they'd do.

"Just because you've been burned once is no reason not to reach for the brass ring again," Ariel said, blithely mixing her metaphors. "Why, Jolene's been married six times. And don't forget, one of those times was to the infamous Peachtree Lane rapist. But that didn't stop her from getting engaged again." Jolene was the headstrong Georgia belle Ariel played on *Southern Nights.*

Feeling decidedly reckless, Sabrina unzipped the dress, stepping into it before common sense prevailed and she changed her mind. "If marriage is such a dandy institution, why don't you get married?"

"We are talkin' about you, sugar," Ariel replied in Jolene's sugary Southern drawl. "And besides, if a man like Prince Burke ever proposed, I'd get him to the altar pronto, before the man knew what hit him."

"Why don't you just hit him over the head with a club and drag him down the aisle?" Raven suggested.

"Why, that's not such a bad idea." Ariel turned toward Dixie with a bold grin. "Mama, how about after dinner, you and I go looking for a nice sturdy tree limb?"

"You girls are all impossible," Dixie answered with a indulgent smile. "And for your information, I happen to agree with Prince Eduard. Every woman wants grandchildren to spoil."

The teasing conversation had taken an all-too-familiar turn. The three sisters pretended a sudden intense interest in dressing for dinner. And even as her stepmother's words created that now-familiar stab of pain in her heart, Sabrina told herself that it was her own fault for not telling the rest of the family the truth about her condition.

At the time, she hadn't wanted their sympathy. Then, like all lies, once told, it had taken on a life of its own, and although now she'd love to have a chance to talk about her emotional pain with her mother and sisters, unfortunately she couldn't quite work up the nerve to confess that she'd been less than truthful.

As she descended the wide curving staircase with Dixie and her sisters, Sabrina vowed to get the dark secret off her chest before the tour ended.

For the first time since her arrival, Burke had joined the family for predinner cocktails. Sabrina knew she was in trouble when her stomach fluttered at the sight of him, resplendent in stark black-and-white evening wear, standing beside the massive stone fireplace.

Reminding herself that discretion was the better part of valor, she remained on the opposite side of the room and was chatting with Chantal when Burke appeared beside her.

"If you don't mind," he said to his sister, "there's something I'd like to show Sabrina."

Chantal arched an ebony brow. "Then I'd suggest you ask her." She gave Sabrina a "men, whatever can you do with them?" look.

"Mademoiselle?" Burke addressed Sabrina for the first time since she'd entered the room ten minutes earlier. His inviting smile made her uneasy.

"It wouldn't be polite of me to be late for dinner."

"This won't take more than a few minutes."

He glanced down at his wafer-thin gold watch. Her father had had a watch like that. Dixie had bought it for him for their twentieth anniversary. It had been ridiculously expensive, Sabrina recalled. She also remembered that Sonny had lost it six months later while fishing for catfish.

"I promise to return you to the dining room with time to spare."

Aware that everyone was watching them, Sabrina told herself that she would have left this room with the devil himself in order to escape all those intent gazes.

"All right, then. I suppose I could spare a few minutes."

Burke's lips quirked. "Thank you," he said formally. "I appreciate your sacrifice."

He took her elbow in his hand and led her from the library and down a maze of curving stairways and high-ceilinged halls.

He entered a room that could have easily doubled as a museum. Sabrina stopped in her tracks and stared at the numerous displays of gleaming armor.

"You brought me here to show me weapons?" That was a distinct surprise. She'd thought he intended to steal a kiss. Or two. Or more. Apparently she'd been wrong.

"Not exactly."

"Good." She folded her arms across her gilded bodice and glanced around. "I suppose this is where I tell you that I'm a pacifist."

"An admirable trait," he agreed easily. "However, in defense of my ancestors, I feel the need to point out that fighting and hunting were once necessary pastimes."

She stopped before a boldly embossed, lavishly etched and gilded set of armor. The silver suit was more than protection against enemy soldiers, she realized. It was a status symbol, meant to dazzle.

"This is quite something." A picture flashed unbidden through her mind: Burke clad in this very armor, astride a gleaming white steed, the sun glinting off the polished silver with a light so bright as to be blinding.

"It belonged to Maximillian I," Burke revealed. "When my grandfather was a child, he collected toy soldiers. As he grew older, the soldiers grew."

"My father collected early Western guns," Sabrina revealed.

"I'd like to see them." Like most Europeans, Burke had a fascination of the American west.

"Mother sold them." Two of his Colt pistols had recently sold at auction in New York and an 1876 Winchester rifle had been bought by a wildcatter who'd struck it rich in the West Texas oil fields before the bust. Dixie, who'd always been vocal about her personal dislike for guns, had cried copious tears when the rifle had sold. Sabrina sighed at the unhappy memory. "She didn't want to. But she didn't have a choice."

Realizing that he was behaving impulsively again, Burke decided to locate Sonny Darling's collection and return it to the man's family. He tried to tell himself that his decision was not due to his feelings for Sabrina, but merely an understanding of tradition and the belief that certain things, no matter their monetary cost, were far more valuable as family keepsakes.

"I didn't invite you here to bring up unpleasant memories," he said. "Rather, I wanted you to see this."

Cupping her elbow in his hand, he led her across the tartan flooring to the opposite wall. There, resplendently surrounded by a heavy gilt frame, hung a life-size full-length portrait of a young woman clad in a traditional scarlet flamenco dress trimmed in an ebony lace flounce. Her dark hair was a wild tangle around her bare shoulders, and her eyes—more black than brown—flashed with tempestuous fire.

"She's absolutely stunning."

"That's Katia Giraudeau, Phillipe's Spanish wife. And my grandmother."

"The gypsy." Sabrina looked into the expressive face and imagined she could hear the staccato clatter of castanets, smell the smoke of the fire.

"Katia was born with second sight," Burke divulged. "Unfortunately Montacroix has always had its share of superstitious citizens, and a few of them accused her of being a witch. Her family, however, learned to trust her uncanny intuition."

Sabrina studied the picture, her attention riveted on those flashing dark gypsy eyes. "Do you believe in clairvoyance?"

Burke shrugged. "It's an intriguing notion, but entirely unsubstantiated by evidence. However," he surprisingly revealed, "although intellectually, I find extrasensory perception difficult to explain, having grown up with Katia as a grandmother, I can't deny the possibility."

Burke decided not to mention that his half sister

Noel had inherited their grandmother's gift. Such personal information was Noel's to share.

"Well, it's certainly a wonderfully vivid portrait."

"It is, isn't it? From the night you arrived, I have been thinking of how much Katia reminds me of you. Which is why I wanted you to see the painting."

It was also a not-very-subtle excuse to get Sabrina alone. Away from her sisters and mother and his family and the bodyguards that constantly hovered around them all.

"Me?" Sabrina glanced at him in surprise. "We don't look anything alike."

"Perhaps you don't resemble each other physically," he allowed. "But you both possess the same fire," he said in a husky tone, "the same energy, the same joie de vivre." *The same dangerous ability to stir a man's blood.*

Sabrina let out a long breath.

"I have been remiss," Burke said.

"Oh?" Her mouth was suddenly very, very dry.

"I failed to tell you how lovely you look tonight." A sheath of gold lamé skimmed her body; the side slits revealed her long and shapely legs.

"Thank you."

He wished he'd been in her bedroom, when she'd performed her predinner rituals—those feminine tricks with creams and scents designed to entice a man.

"Monique informed Chantal that you sent her away earlier this evening."

Tattletale, Sabrina thought. She was also discomfited to learn that Burke and his sister had been talking about her.

"Monique is very efficient and very nice, but when she wanted to draw my bath, I merely suggested that she find something else to occupy her time."

"Drawing your bath is part of her duty."

"I realize that. I just didn't like it."

"You don't like servants?"

"Of course I do. And I'm sure I'd come to like Monique, once I got to know her. It's having her hovering around, waiting on me that makes me nervous."

"Most women in my experience enjoy being waited on."

She tilted her chin. Her gray eyes darkened to the hue of a stormy sea. "I feel obliged to point out that is a highly sexist remark, Your Highness. Besides, I'm not most women."

"No." He gave her a long considering look. "You are most definitely not."

Their gazes met in a flash of shared intimacy like nothing Burke had ever known. As he struggled to regain control of himself and the situation, he tried to remember who—and what he was.

When she felt her face growing warm, Sabrina tried to lower her gaze, but couldn't.

It was as if his dark eyes were undressing her mind and she was powerless to resist.

"Don't you think we should be getting back to the dining room, Your Highness?" Although it took every ounce of restraint she possessed, she didn't back away.

"Don't you think it's time you dropped the formality and called me Burke?"

Giving in to temptation, he cupped her chin in his fingers and brushed his thumb over her delicate jawline, pleased when Sabrina didn't flinch or turn away.

"What is it about you?" he murmured. "What dark magic do you possess that makes me unable to get you out of my mind?"

While she was attempting to come up with an answer to that startling question, he slowly, deliberately lowered his head. All it took was the warm flutter of his breath to make Sabrina's lips part and her concentration waver.

And then he touched his lips to hers. Testing. Tasting.

Sabrina never would have expected that his firm, uncompromising mouth could be so tender. Or feel so right. She sighed in soft, shimmering pleasure even as she told herself she should not allow this.

He used no pressure. No power. Only soft, patient persuasion. His hands moved up her bare arms, creating a trail of heat before cupping her face between his palms.

"I knew it," he murmured. His long fingers combed through her hair, tilting her head so he could look deep into her eyes.

"Knew what?" His gaze was making her knees weak; seeking support, she grasped on to his broad shoulders.

"That you would taste every bit as good as you looked."

Gently, and with infinite care, his lips plucked at hers, tempting, teasing, soothing Sabrina's tension and making her forget all her reasons why this was wrong.

And then slowly, degree by glorious degree, he deepened the kiss, drawing it out until she linked her fingers around his neck, closed her eyes and let her body meld to his.

Urgency rose; desire flared. Her soft lips moved avidly, instinctively beneath his, her arms wrapped around him and clung. They both felt it—the need to touch. And be touched.

It was no longer a tentative, exploratory first kiss. Feelings flared. Emotions erupted.

When Burke's lips skimmed up her face to loiter at her temple, she sighed. When they pressed against the ragged pulse at the base of her throat, she moaned. And when he brushed a series of stinging kisses along the ridge of her collarbone, she moaned again and clung.

He'd stopped thinking. In some distant corner of his mind, Burke told himself that he was in danger of risking everything for this one fleeting moment's insanity. Even as he warned himself that his behavior was sheer madness, he found himself wanting more.

More, she thought, as his tongue slid seductively over hers. A jagged need sliced through her. Every pore of her body seemed to be crying out with it. Desperation pounded in her, hot and heavy, with each heartbeat. She wanted—needed—more. So very much more.

His lips burned their way down her throat, his hand skimmed down her back to find some hitherto undiscovered point near the base of her backbone. A perfectly placed finger pressing against it caused flames to shoot up her spine.

"No. Please." Sabrina drew in a quick, harsh breath as the deep-seated instinct for survival finally kicked in.

Pulling free, she dragged an unsteady hand through her now-tumbled hair and stared at him.

"I think we'd better rejoin the others," she insisted quietly.

Need roared inside him; Burke struggled for calm. Another minute and she would have had him on his knees. He wanted to curse her for making him feel like a teenager; he wanted to rip that little gold dress away and take her here and now, satisfying the hunger that had tormented both body and mind for days.

"Whatever you wish." His dark eyes took a slow tour of her flushed face. Burke tried to remember when any woman had taken him so far, so deep, with merely a kiss, and came up blank. "Should I apologize?"

Her eyes flashed with renewed spirit. "Don't you dare."

"*Bien*. I won't." Burke had never begged for a woman; with Sabrina he feared that begging might be inevitable. It might also be worth it. "Would it make you feel safer if I gave you my word that I will be on my best behavior for the remainder of the evening?"

"Perhaps."

She could trust him, Sabrina determined as they returned to the dining room. But what about herself?

They'd just finished dinner when Burke surprised Sabrina once again.

"Madame Darling," he said, addressing Dixie, who was seated at the end of the table, to Eduard's right, "I feel that having been so immersed in my preparations for the race, I have been neglecting my hosting duties. It would be my honor if you—and your lovely daughters, of course—permitted me to escort you to the casino this evening."

Sonny had teased his wife of single-handedly keeping Nashville's Our Lady of Mercy Catholic church afloat with her unwavering devotion to the parish's Wednesday-night bingo games. That being the case, Sabrina was not surprised when Dixie's face lighted up like a Christmas tree at the prince's suggestion.

"Why, the honor would be ours, Your Highness."

Raven and Ariel also expressed a desire to visit the renowned playground of the world's rich and famous.

Which left Sabrina to demur.

"Don't you have some official function to attend?"

"There was a prerace cocktail party," he agreed. "And some mention of a late-night get-together. But

I'm certain that the other drivers and their guests will muddle through quite well without me."

"But you have another time trial tomorrow."

"*Oui.* But the car is in perfect running order. There is nothing left for me to do but to show up on time."

"I'd think you'd want a good night's sleep."

"It is still early. And some time at the tables will undoubtedly relax me."

But Sabrina knew that time spent with the playboy prince would prove anything but relaxing for her. She was about to pass on the entire idea when she saw the faintest flicker of a challenge in Burke's dark eyes. It was a mirror of the one she'd tossed his way earlier today.

"I don't gamble."

"Everyone gambles," Burke argued easily.

"I don't."

"Life is a gamble."

"Not mine." She could feel the interested gazes of the two families watching her exchange with Burke. She also knew she was being unreasonably uncooperative, but couldn't seem to stop herself.

He looked at her for a long, silent time, his dark eyes inscrutable. "Then perhaps it is time that you took a risk."

And he was not referring to any game found in the casino.

"I wouldn't know how to play the game." She too, was not referring to baccarat or roulette, but to whatever was happening between her and the prince.

Burke nodded his silent acceptance of her complaint. "That is easily overcome. Our croupiers are extremely helpful."

He had just deftly cut off her escape route.

"It sounds delightful," she said, lying through her

teeth. Her tone was that of a woman who knew that to resist any longer would be to invite speculation.

"Parfait," Burke said. His tone was that of a man totally accustomed to getting his way.

For not the first time since meeting Montacroix's prince, Sabrina was left with the impression that although he possessed a great deal more charm than her former husband, in his own way, Burke Giraudeau was every bit as controlling.

LIKE EVERYTHING ELSE in the country, the royal casino—with its rococo turrets and green copper cupolas illuminated by bright spotlights—could have come from the illustrated pages of a fairy tale.

As he escorted the quartet up the marble steps, Burke stopped before a bronze statue of a man in full battle dress seated astride a prancing stallion.

"This is Prince Léon," he revealed. "He is the reason that our detractors claim that we have more statues in Montacroix than we do citizens. That is, of course, an exaggeration. However, during his reign, more than two hundred statues were commissioned. It is impossible to drive through the countryside without seeing one of Léon's statues."

"The pigeons must love him," Sabrina said dryly.

Burke smiled. "My own feelings, exactly. Custom has it that rubbing the knee of Léon's horse will bring one luck."

"Well," Ariel drawled, reaching out a perfectly manicured hand to stroke the burnished bronze horse, "far be it from me to buck custom."

Dixie followed her daughter's example, as did Raven, although her expression suggested that she was far too sensible for such superstition and was merely humoring the others.

"Sabrina?" Burke invited with an arched brow.

Some perverse instinct had her resist his request. "I've always believed in making my own luck."

When her lovely, stubborn jaw pointed his way again, Burke's fingers practically itched with the desire to curl around it and hold its owner to another one of those mind-blinding kisses. With a self-control that was rapidly slipping away, like sands between his fingers, he managed, with a Herculean effort, to resist.

"Once again we are in perfect accord," he said on a husky voice that affected her nearly as much as his earlier kiss.

Accustomed to the bright lights and glitter of Las Vegas or Atlantic City, where Sonny had so often headlined, the Montacroix casino had an old-fashioned, upper-class atmosphere.

Hand-cut prisms of crystal chandeliers sparkled from the ceiling, so unlike the garish neon usually associated with American casinos. The arched ceilings boasted gilt frescoes, and priceless Impressionist paintings adorned the walls of the softly lighted salons where stunningly beautiful, silk clad female croupiers oversaw games of roulette, blackjack and baccarat. The marble-patterned carpeting continued the elegance of the Italian marble foyer, while muffling the sounds in the vast room.

The gamblers, too, were different from the eclectic mix of Americans who frequented the Nevada and New Jersey casinos. In those gambling halls, one could find gamblers dressed in everything from faded jeans to expensive designer original evening gowns, all pressed together in absolute equality.

Here, democracy had been abandoned for an atmosphere of elegant chic where the world's highest rollers risked the odd few million while deciding what European hotel or department store to buy next. The women wore their exquisite jewels proudly and openly, something they were no longer safe to do in so many of the other European playgrounds. Although not one to keep up on the comings and goings of the glitterati, Sabrina recognized several celebrities.

There were no exuberant cries of victory as fortunes were won, no mournful cries or shouted expletives as others were lost. There was only the steady hum of subdued, cultured voices.

The main gallery shushed as Burke passed through with his guests. Following in their wake was the hum of murmured curious voices. From the way he'd placed his hand lightly on her back, ostensibly guiding her through the throng of gamblers, Sabrina suspected that much of that interest was directed toward her.

"This is the *Salon Privé*," Burke informed the little group as they entered a room that was smaller, but even more exquisitely decorated than the main gallery.

When he smiled toward a lovely young blonde in her early twenties, clad in a long black beaded sheath that hugged every voluptuous curve, Sabrina felt that same unwelcome stab of jealousy she'd experienced when she'd seen the newspaper photo of the prince with Princess Caroline.

The woman glided across the vermilion-and-gold carpeting, somehow managing, despite the snugness of her gown, a perfect curtsy. "Your Highness," she greeted him in French-accented English. "I've arranged things for your guests, exactly as you've requested."

"*Bien*." His pleased smile was warm, admiring and intimate. Sabrina hated the woman without even knowing her. "I've arranged for each of you to have a credit with the bank."

The overly generous amount he stated drew surprised, pleased gasps from Dixie, Raven and Ariel. But not Sabrina. She had already decided that there was nothing Prince Burke could do that would surprise her. And although it was an unpalatable thought, Sabrina also suspected that such generosity was merely a way to buy Dixie's compliance for a dalliance with the eldest Darling daughter.

If that was his plan, it was definitely working. After turning the others over to the beautiful salon hostess he'd introduced as Dominique, he turned to Sabrina.

"Since you stated you don't gamble, I will be pleased to assist you in learning the game."

"Oh, isn't that nice," Dixie enthused. "Go along, Sabrina, darling. And have a good time." From her mother's overt delight, as well as the amused expression on both her sisters' faces, Sabrina realized that she was not going to receive any help from that quarter.

"All right," she grumbled as she allowed herself to be guided to the far side of the salon. "But I hope you won't be too annoyed when I lose every franc."

Burke stopped, gazed down at her for a heart stoppingly long time, then ran the back of his hand down her cheek. "I doubt that there is anything you could do to annoy me, Sabrina."

A silken net had drifted over them. They could have been the only two people in the room.

The mere touch of his hand against her skin had turned her mouth as arid as an Arabian desert. Sabrina had a sudden urge to lick her dry lips. An urge she resisted.

"You never know," she quipped on a shaky voice. "The night's still young."

He laughed at that, another one of those deep rich

laughs that thankfully succeeded in breaking the seductive spell.

"Come along with me, Sabrina," he said, leading her toward the roulette wheel. "For some reason, tonight I am feeling very lucky."

6

THE FEMALE CROUPIER dipped into a curtsy when Burke stopped at her wheel, then placed a pile of chips in front of Sabrina. After explaining that unlike the multicolored chips used in America, European roulette used only a single color, Burke invited her to choose a number.

"There are so many." Sabrina bit her lip. Although the plastic chips didn't seem like real money, for some reason the decision seemed vastly important. The other gamblers, along with the tuxedo-clad woman at the wheel, waited patiently for Sabrina's turn. Any guest of the royal family could take all night and there would not be so much as a whisper of complaint.

"Why don't you start by choosing a color," Burke suggested. "There are only two choices."

That was easy. Sabrina chose red, the color of Burke's dangerous-looking race car.

"A reckless woman," he chuckled when she placed a single chip on the expanse of green felt. "At least this way it should take all night for you to lose all these chips." The idea of spending the night with the lovely Sabrina was decidedly appealing, although Burke could think of far more pleasant ways to pass the time than playing roulette.

"Shh," she hissed as the wheel began to spin. "I'm trying to concentrate." She didn't take her eyes from the bouncing steel ball, which eventually fell into the slot occupied by the red number twelve.

"I won!" She clapped her hands as the banker returned her chip, along with another one. "Oh, I'm going to do it again!"

Ignoring his amused glance, she placed another single chip on black, the color of Burke's gleaming dark hair. She held her breath, every muscle in her body tense as the wheel spun round and round, the ball finally settling into the black number one.

They couldn't lose. It was as if some benevolent genie were perched on Sabrina's bare shoulder. As the night went on, Sabrina grew more lionhearted, moving on to numbers, playing hunches, winning every time. The pile of chips grew.

It was much, much later when she finally came down to earth. A brunette waitress, clad in a black Grecian-style gown, appeared at Burke's elbow, with two flutes of champagne.

"Dominique sent this wine to celebrate your guest's good fortune," she said with a smile.

"Thank you." Burke took the glasses with what Sabrina was beginning to recognize as his official royal smile. "Please tell Dominique that we appreciate the gesture."

He handed a glass to Sabrina. "I believe a toast is in order."

Wanting to share her good fortune, Sabrina was puzzled when she couldn't catch sight of her sisters or her mother.

"Where are the others?"

"They returned to the palace an hour ago."

"An hour ago?" Sabrina looked down at her watch, shocked to see that it was past midnight. "Why didn't they tell me they were leaving?"

"Your mother didn't want to chance breaking your lucky streak."

"Oh." That made sense, Sabrina admitted. Dixie had always been incredibly superstitious. "Well, we'd better be going as well. After all, you do have to race in just a few hours."

"Whatever you wish." His planned toast forgotten, Burke placed the untouched champagne on the tray of a passing waiter. "I'll cash in these chips."

While he went to the gilded barred window, Sabrina idly glanced around the room, surprised to recognize Burke's American chauffeur seated at the bar.

"Your chauffeur seems to be making the most of his time," she said when Burke returned.

"Drew never gambles while on duty," Burke said mildly. "Nor does he drink. Hold out your hand."

The chauffeur was immediately forgotten as Burke counted into her palm the stack of colorful bills vaguely reminiscent of Monopoly money.

"What in the world is all this?"

"Your winnings."

She stared down at the money. "How much, exactly, did I win?"

"About one hundred thousand Montacroix francs."

Shock waves reverberated through her. "What's that in American money?"

"Somewhere in the neighborhood of seventy-five thousand dollars. Actually, a bit more than that."

"That's some neighborhood. How in the world did I win so much?"

"It's not hard to do when you're playing with hundred-franc chips."

"Those were hundred-franc chips?" she repeated on a squeak. Fool that she was, she'd never thought to ask.

It was Burke's turn to look surprised. "Of course. What did you think they were?"

"I don't know. Five francs. Perhaps ten."

"In Montacroix?" Burke asked, clearly amused at her naïveté.

Sabrina thrust the colorful paper money toward him. "I can't keep this."

"Of course you can." He took the bills, unfastened the clasp of her evening purse and stuffed them inside. "If the idea of spending it on yourself is a problem, consider it my contribution to the Sonny Darling tax-relief fund. Besides," he added, "don't forget, you could have just as easily lost it all."

Her knees weakened at that idea. That had always been one of the reasons she never gambled. She'd accompanied her husband and his friends innumerable times on junkets to Atlantic City, where glitter brightened the night sky and the smoky air was static with expectation, desperation and tragedy.

Sabrina had already chosen a chancy career; that was all the risk she felt prepared to handle in one life.

BEHIND THE CASINO, a man and a woman met in the shadows.

"You failed." His voice was coldly angry; his eyes resembled hard black stones.

"It wasn't my fault." She was trembling, not from the night air but from a very real fear. "He took the drugged champagne, just as you said he would, but then that American woman wanted to leave, and—"

The man's curse was quick and harsh. "You will forget everything about tonight." He reached into his pocket and took out a pair of black leather driving gloves. "You will erase from your mind the fact that you've ever met me."

"Yes. I will." Her eyes were riveted on his hands as he pulled on the gloves. "I promise. I will forget everything."

His smile flashed in the muted light with the deadly intent of a stiletto. "Yes," the man agreed as he ran one hand down her ashen cheek. "You will definitely forget everything."

His fingers trailed down her face, then her neck. Sensing his intent, the woman tried to flee, but she was too frightened to move quickly, and her attacker was too intent on his deadly mission. His black gloved fingers curled around her throat. And then he squeezed, strangling off her attempted scream for help. Her eyes grew wide and terrified, her face lost all its color. And then, she slumped to the ground.

The man stood there, eyeing her slender feminine body sprawled lifelessly on the wet dark cobblestones.

"Such a waste," he murmured. His fleeting expression of regret quickly faded, replaced with renewed determination. Then, pocketing the gloves, he disappeared into the Montacroix night.

SABRINA'S MIND was still spinning with thoughts of how Dixie was going to react to this unexpected windfall as they climbed into the back seat of the limousine. It had begun to rain; a steady drizzle that diffused the lights lining the street.

"I don't know how to thank you," she murmured.

"If you feel the need to thank someone, thank Lady Luck. I was just along for the ride."

His gesture was more than generous, she mused as she looked out the window. And the way he'd suggested she use her winnings to help pay off the IRS debt proved that he understood—and shared—her intense loyalty to family.

A lone man, clad in a black leather trench coat and slouch hat was walking briskly along the sidewalk. For a moment, when he glanced toward the passing limousine, Sabrina thought their eyes met. But that was impossible, she reminded herself. The windows of the limousine were heavily tinted. But that didn't prevent her from studying him as the limo paused at a red light.

His face was lean and angular, his mouth thin, his eyes sunken deep beneath protruding brows. There was something about those black eyes—something cold and foreboding—that made her shiver.

"Are you all right?" Burke asked, seeing her slight tremor. "If you're cold, I can have the driver turn up the heat."

"No." Sabrina dragged her gaze from the stranger's stony face. "A cat just walked over my grave."

"A cat?"

"It's an expression." As the light turned green and the limousine continued on its way, she shook off the strange, uneasy feeling and managed a faint smile that only wobbled slightly. "Describing a feeling...like ice up your spine."

"Ah. That I know," Burke agreed. "Was it something I said that brought on this feeling?"

"No," she said truthfully, deciding not to reveal her odd premonition. "It was probably just fatigue. And excitement from the gambling."

"Perhaps," Burke agreed. But he didn't look fully convinced. Instead, Sabrina considered, he looked genuinely concerned. She found such honest regard for her feelings even more dangerous than the fact that he was a dynamite kisser.

"You're not at all what I expected," she admitted softly.

Her scent—an erotic perfume suggestive of sex and sin—had been driving him to distraction all night. "What were you expecting?"

"I don't know," she hedged, not wanting to ruin a lovely night by admitting to her own prejudices. "It's difficult to put into words," she murmured, pretending a sudden interest in the scenery outside the window.

"Let me try," Burke suggested. "How about self-indulgent, egocentric, hedonistic. An unprincipled playboy. An oversexed libertine without conscience or scruples. Am I getting warm?"

Actually, he'd hit the nail precisely on its head. "Something like that," Sabrina mumbled, feeling increasingly uncomfortable. "Except I hadn't thought of 'libertine.'"

"Given a bit more time, I'm sure it would have occurred to you," Burke said easily. "So, with the danger of having my ego deflated even further, what do you think of me now?"

She turned toward him, surprised to find that he'd moved closer. Their faces were little more than a whisper apart.

"I think," she said slowly, "that you are a very complex man."

"A fairly accurate assessment," he agreed. "Which I suppose isn't all that surprising, coming from an equally complex woman."

"But I'm not at all complex."

He lifted a disbelieving brow. "Aren't you?"

"Of course not. Why, everyone has always said that I was the most extroverted of Sonny Darling's three daughters."

"You are the best actress," Burke corrected. "But while you are flamboyantly displaying whatever it is you want people to believe, you work overtime at keeping your true feelings hidden away, bottled up deep inside you. Which isn't always successful, because your remarkable eyes give you away."

Only with him, Sabrina could have told him, but didn't. Although she was, admittedly, an emotional person, others only saw what she wanted them to see. During the past four days, Sabrina had come to the conclusion that Burke was an intelligent man. Now she realized he was insightful as well.

"You should have told me that you inherited Katia's gift for second sight."

"I didn't. The truth is, Sabrina, that you and I are a great deal alike. We wear our public masks in much the same way my ancestors once wore those protective suits of armor you saw earlier this evening. Having both suffered feelings of abandonment as children, we've built walls around ourselves. But there is something I believe you have yet to learn."

She desperately wanted to argue. To deny everything he was saying. But she couldn't. Because it was all true.

"What's that?" she asked on a whisper.

His long fingers encircled her chin, holding her wary gaze to his. "The same walls so painstakingly erected to keep others out, also keep us in. And before long, we find ourselves in a prison of our own making."

He was so close. Too close. She put her palms against his chest, intending, if not exactly to push him away, to at least hold him at bay. "I'm not—"

"Oh, yes, you are," he insisted, cutting off her planned denial. His thumb stroked a line of sparks around her lips. "Lower the drawbridge, Sabrina." Bending his dark head, he brushed his mouth against hers, silkily, enticingly. "Let yourself feel again."

His lips were soft and warm and so exquisitely gentle that Sabrina felt herself melting into the glove-soft leather seat. Once again Burke had surprised her: she'd been expecting an instantaneous flare of dangerous passion. But instead his gentleness was shattering her defenses, crumbling her parapets, in ways that hot masculine demands never could.

Her hands clutched at his pleated white dress shirt, her head fell back in surrender, and her lips parted, inviting the sweet invasion of his tongue.

Kissing Sabrina was like falling into a sensual dream from which he never wanted to awaken. His hands tangled in her hair, scattering pins, ripping apart the artfully simplistic coiffure that had taken Ariel nearly an hour to create.

Burke sensed Sabrina's surrender, and instead of feeling victorious, he was humbled by her willingness to trust so completely. To give so openly.

With a pang of regret, he broke the leisurely kiss long enough to lean forward and push a button on the console. "We'll be taking the long way back to the palace, driver."

Drew Tremayne, displaying properly servile demeanor, did not even glance up at the rearview mirror. "Yes, Your Highness," he replied blandly.

Burke pushed another button, causing the thick tinted glass to rise between the front and back seats.

When he turned back to Sabrina, the sight of her momentarily took his breath away. Her golden hair was tousled from his fingers, her lips were parted invitingly, and her eyes were wide and clouded and, he noticed reluctantly, unsure.

For one brief, fleeting moment, his mind brought forth a picture of Sabrina lying in a sun-kissed bed of wild buttercups, her catlike eyes smiling up at him, her arms outstretched.

Forcing the evocative image away, Burke ran his knuckles down her flushed cheek in a slow, tender sweep. "I promise, *chérie,* I will not hurt you."

Even as she knew Burke honestly meant those gravely stated words, Sabrina knew he was wrong. Because he would hurt her. Oh, he wouldn't mean to. But whatever happened between them tonight, they would have no choice but to part. She would resume the tour designed to salvage her father's reputation while he would remain here, where he belonged, in Montacroix.

In six short days, Burke would become regent. And Sabrina had come to know enough about him to accept the fact that in time, he would do his duty to his family and country by choosing a proper wife capable of giving him the heirs necessary to ensure the continuation of the Montacroix principality.

Oh, he might think of her from time to time, she considered. But eventually she'd fade from his mind like a distant dream. Or a summer dalliance with an appealing American commoner.

Every ounce of common sense Sabrina possessed told her that she should back away from this temptation, now. Before it was too late for choice.

But as his caressing hand moved down her cheek, and then her throat, creating a terrible pitch of excitement in her blood, Sabrina knew it had been too late from the beginning. From that first moment she'd found herself drowning in his smoky dark eyes.

"I don't want to talk," she said, raking her hands through his crisp black hair and pulling his mouth back to hers. *I don't want to think.* Her avid lips plucked hungrily at his, her kiss hot and hungry. Her slender hands, naked of any jeweled adornment, clutched at his hair, bringing his mouth back to hers, again and again.

When her teeth plucked at the cord in his neck, need punched like a fist into his gut, surging through Burke's furnace-hot body. His tongue stabbed deeply into her mouth, his greedy hands moved over her, clutching pieces of gold-lamé-covered flesh.

He was no longer gentle, but—for some reason she promised herself to think about later, when her head ceased spinning and her body was no longer aflame— Sabrina did not want gentleness.

Her hands ripped at the starched shirtfront, sending black ebony studs flying. She pushed the material away, her fingers twisting in his black chest hairs as her mouth ate into his.

Need pumping through him, Burke unfastened her gold dress, the zipper sounding unnaturally loud in the close confines of the limo. He yanked the clinging bodice of the gown to her waist, giving his hands access to her breasts.

When he lowered his head and took a taut rosy peak between his teeth and tugged, Sabrina made a low, deep sound in her throat that was half purr, half growl. Pulling her into his arms, he arranged her so that she was lying across his lap. Attempting to regain control, he forced himself to be satisfied with long, slow kisses. Her taste coursed through him like a roiling river, a roaring filled his head. Tension built, and as much as he wanted to bury himself deep in her moist warmth, Burke held back.

She was sprawled wantonly across him, her gold kid shoes on the seat of the car, her skirt riding high on her long legs.

"You are so beautiful." He slipped his hand beneath her skirt and trailed his fingers up her thigh, tracing a seductive pattern that left her trembling. "That first moment I saw you, looking like a ravishing blond gypsy, you took my breath away."

"I felt it, too," she admitted on a throaty voice that was half honey, half smoke. "I didn't want to. But I did."

His lips curved into a satisfied smile that only hours earlier would have irritated her. But now her own ravished lips returned his rakish grin. They smiled at each other for an exquisitely long time.

Underlying the aura of sensuality was a familiarity so strong Burke felt as if he could reach out and touch it. He'd dreamed about her—or someone remarkably like her—for so long that it seemed as if he'd been waiting for her his entire life.

He'd fantasized about horseback riding with her beside the diamond-bright waters of Lake Losange, imagined kissing her in a hidden Alpine grove, dreamed of making love in front of a blazing fire. During these atypical flights of fantasy, when she finally arrived, no words were needed. He'd simply known.

Perhaps, Burke thought with a burst of self-directed humor, he had inherited a smattering of Katia's second sight. Because as a slow flame spread through him anew, it was as if he could read Sabrina's mind; as if their sensual thoughts had tangled.

Burke had never experienced anything like this with any other woman. Any other lover.

It would be so easy, he mused. Another kiss, a touch here, a long, lingering caress there, and he could have her in his arms crying out for release. But then what? What of tomorrow?

As his gaze swept over her softly flushed features, Burke admitted that he wanted a great deal more than a tumble in the back of a limousine.

Dragging his eyes away from Sabrina, he glanced out the steamed-up window. "We're almost at the palace."

"Yes." Her voice was breathy with anticipation.

With hands that were not as steady as he would have liked, Burke reluctantly rearranged her clothing, then nudged her back onto the seat beside him. "I'll walk you to your door. And then I must go to the garage."

"The garage?" She didn't even try to keep the surprise and disappointment from her voice.

"I want to check the car before tomorrow's time trial."

"Oh." His rejection, after the passion they'd shared, felt like a slap in the face. She felt embarrassed and ashamed and couldn't bear to meet his look. "I understand."

"*Non, ma chère,*" he corrected gently, taking her downcast chin and forcing her to look up at him. "I don't believe you do."

"Really, Your Highness—"

"Surely we've progressed to a point where you feel comfortable using my first name."

When she didn't answer, he said, "I want very much to make love to you, Sabrina."

"Of course you do," she returned, her Darling temper flaring to rescue her from humiliation. "That's why you're rushing off to the garage the minute we get back to the palace." Sabrina hated the cold, petulant sound of her own voice. If she'd been reading for a play, the margin notes would have read: *woman scorned.*

"I want to make love to you," he repeated gently, but firmly. To prove his point, he took her hand, which had tightened into a clenched fist in her lap, slowly uncurled her fingers and pressed it against an aching part of his anatomy.

"See what you do to me?" he growled. "All it takes is a single glance of your polished silver eyes, or the musical sound of your laughter, or the merest touch of your slender hand against mine, for my body to betray itself in an embarrassing, painful way."

The frustration in his tone, along with a lingering desire was enough to make her believe him. "Then why?"

He stroked the back of her hand, which was still pressed against his groin, with his fingertip. He couldn't entirely explain his feelings to her because he hadn't succeeded in explaining them to himself. "We will make love, Sabrina. When the time and the place is right. And although I doubt that I shall sleep the rest of this night, I wish to do this properly."

As the limousine pulled beneath the porte cochere, Burke lifted her trembling hand to his lips.

"I do, however, have one request before I behave like the gentleman I wish I wasn't and resist this delightful temptation."

Afraid that she was close to giving Burke whatever he wanted, her eyes turned wary. "What request is that?"

"I would be honored if you would let me take you on the tour of the vineyards tomorrow morning. This morning, actually," he corrected.

An image of making love to Burke amid thick green vines pregnant with lush purple grapes, flashed enticingly through Sabrina's mind. She could smell the rich dark earth mingling with the sweet scent of ripening grapes; she could feel the sunshine warming their flesh. She could see their entwined bodies...

This had to stop! Burke was not just playing havoc

with her body; ever since they'd met, her imagination had gone into overdrive.

"I don't know if that would be a very good idea."

"Please, Sabrina." His lips brushed her knuckles, creating a now-familiar flare of desire.

She let out a long breath as her mind and heart raced. "I wouldn't imagine that 'please' is a word a prince would have to use very often."

"I'm a man, first," he reminded her unnecessarily. "Before I'm a prince. But you are right, I save begging and groveling for the really important occasions."

She tugged her hand free and was about to retort that she hardly considered his request to be either begging or groveling when she saw the relaxed humor in his eyes.

"Are you laughing at me?"

"No." His gaze warmed. "Not exactly."

"What exactly do you find so humorous?"

"Us, I suppose. The situation. This chemistry."

"Chemistry," Sabrina murmured, feeling the heat flooding her cheeks yet again. "Is that a polite term for lust?"

"Whatever you want to call it, Sabrina, you can no longer deny that it exists. Not after tonight."

"No. I can't."

Sabrina had never believed in lying. Not even to herself. Especially to herself. She took another deep breath and felt her equilibrium begin to return.

"I don't understand. I'm usually much more circumspect in my relationships with men." She hated Burke thinking that she literally threw herself into the arms of every handsome man who came along. In truth, she hadn't been with a man since her marriage disintegrated.

And even before she'd caught him in bed with her

understudy, she and her husband had maintained separate bedrooms for months. In the beginning, he'd professed not to want to hurt her after her surgery. In the end, Sabrina came to realize that it had only been an excuse not to make love to her. Which wasn't that surprising. She'd always known, from their debacle of a Caribbean honeymoon, that she was incapable of satisfying an intensely sexual man such as her husband.

So what made her think she could satisfy this man? she asked herself now. That idea, which had not occurred to her while she'd been burning in the prince's arms, was horribly depressing.

The passionate mood had passed and Burke, for the time being, was relieved. "Perhaps it was my smooth, continental charm that was nearly your undoing."

Dragging her mind back to their conversation, Sabrina chewed on a crimson fingernail and eyed him thoughtfully. "I don't think so."

"My devastatingly dark looks?"

"Sorry."

"How about the fact that I am first in line to the royal throne of the principality of Montacroix?"

"What on earth would that have to do with anything?"

On the contrary, it was the main reason she felt so threatened by her feelings for him. With any other man, she may have allowed herself to hope. To risk. But with this man—this prince—Sabrina knew there could be no future.

"I have heard of something called a Cinderella complex, which states that despite what they say, all women secretly wish for a Prince Charming to sweep them off their feet, take them away from their boring, humdrum lives to his palace, where they and all the little princes and princesses will live happily ever after."

He'd hit a little too close to home. Memories of her long-ago fantasies danced enticingly through her mind. Sabrina stubbornly ignored them.

"Not that I believe in that ridiculous bit of pop psychobabble in the first place, even if I did, I'd be forced to point out that my life—both professionally and personally—is far from humdrum, Your Highness."

A smile tugged at the corners of his mouth. "I'll readily agree with your professional acclaim, Sabrina. As for your far-from-humdrum love life, I suppose I'll just have to take your word on that."

"You do that." Despite her lingering feelings of desire, Sabrina was amused by the deft way he'd managed to lighten the unsettling sensual mood. "So with my enviable professional acclaim, not to mention all those men waiting at the stage door, what could I possibly need with a prince?"

"What indeed?" Although he was determined to give her some space, Burke couldn't resist touching her. Her hair, free of its pins, tumbled nearly to her waist.

Reaching out, he ran his palm down the silken waves. "You should always wear your hair down."

The masculine possessiveness in his tone rankled. "Is that a royal command, Your Highness?"

"Not a royal command." Without bothering to seek her permission, he captured several gilt strands and sifted them like grains of gleaming sand through his fingers. "Merely a man's request."

His words, his gaze, his touch, pleased her and Sabrina didn't even try to hide it. "With lines like that, it's no wonder that you have every woman on the continent chasing after you."

It was, unfortunately, all too true. There had of course been women. Many of them. Perhaps even too many in his youth. As he'd grown older he'd realized that several women had wanted nothing more than the thrill of going to bed with royalty. When that realization struck home, he became a great deal more choosy.

And Burke didn't want every woman on the continent. He wanted Sabrina.

"The press exaggerates. As I am sure you know all too well."

Sabrina thought back on all the cruel, fictional stories that had been written about Sonny over the years. She certainly hadn't escaped, either. In fact, if she'd had a dollar for every time some supermarket tabloid had put her father or her on the cover, she'd be able to move into one of those exclusive Park Avenue apartments with a view of Central Park.

"Point taken," she murmured. "Well, I'd better be getting upstairs."

Knowing that if they stayed together any longer, all his good intentions would dissolve like a sand castle at high tide, Burke didn't argue.

"I really did have a wonderful evening," she said into the relaxed silence surrounding them as they lingered once again at the door to her suite.

"You sound surprised."

"I suppose I am."

Even as he would have preferred a polite little lie, Burke found himself admiring her truthfulness. "We didn't get off to a very auspicious start," he admitted. "And I suppose the blame for that lies with me."

"Not with you." She leaned her head back against the silk-covered wall. "It was just a…" Sabrina's voice trailed off. The long day, the excitement of the gambling, the heated kisses she'd shared with Burke in the back of the limousine, all conspired to make her suddenly exhausted. "Strange situation," she murmured, willing her weary brain to come up with a proper explanation.

"You know we're going to have to talk about it," Burke said quietly. There was something important happening between them. Undercurrents they would not be able to ignore for very long.

Sabrina didn't want to hear Burke list all the sane, practical reasons why he couldn't offer her a future. She suspected that as the gentleman she now knew him to be, he would feel obligated to tell her there was nothing permanent about their relationship. That if she chose to make love to him, it would only be an affair.

"Tomorrow," she murmured on a sultry Southern drawl. "At Tara." Linking her hands around his neck, Sabrina lifted her face for Burke's good-night kiss and allowed herself to risk.

7

THE FOLLOWING MORNING, Burke stood in the basement of the Montacroix Police Station, frowning down at the lifeless form that only last night had been a vibrant, attractive young woman.

"Yes, I recognize her," he said quietly. "She worked at the casino. She was a waitress in the *Salon Privé*."

"The casino manager claims never to have seen her," Caine informed him.

Burke shot him a quick, surprised look. "But that's impossible. Only last night this same woman brought Sabrina and me each a glass of champagne. She claimed it was from Dominique, to celebrate Sabrina's luck at the tables."

Caine's dark eyes narrowed. "What time would that have been?"

"After midnight," Burke answered promptly.

"That'd be a bit difficult," Drew said. He'd accompanied Burke to the old brick building. "Since Dominique went home early last night. She'd already left the casino by eleven-thirty."

Burke snapped to attention. "Impossible."

"Her story checks out," Caine said. "Apparently her mother was taken ill. The casino telephone operator logged the call at eleven-twenty."

"Her mother has a heart condition," Burke remembered. "That was the reason Dominique moved in with her last month. To ensure that she was being properly taken care of." His dark brow furrowed. "How is Madame Brasseur?"

"According to the doctors at the hospital, it was only a slight flutter. She was kept overnight for observation and released this morning."

"That, at least, is good news." Burke made a mental note to send the elderly woman flowers and have the casino manager instruct Dominique to take all the time she needed before returning to work. With pay, of course.

"And her daughter stayed by her side all night," Drew tacked on significantly.

"Then Dominique could not possibly have sent the champagne," Burke considered.

"Not unless she called the order in from the emergency room," Caine concurred. "And although the casino manager assured me that Dominique Brasseur is a model employee, she undoubtedly had something more important on her mind than ensuring her boss celebrated his guest's good fortune. Did you drink any of the champagne?"

As Burke remembered placing the untouched glasses on the passing tray, ice skimmed up his spine, reminding him of something Sabrina had said last night. A cat walking over her grave.

At this moment, looking down at the poor unfortunate woman laid out unceremoniously on the stainless steel table, he understood the American idiom perfectly.

"No. Sabrina was fatigued. She wished to return to the palace."

"Lucky for you," Drew murmured.

"Damn lucky," Caine concurred.

"I don't suppose you will be able to locate those glasses," Burke asked. What if one of the drinks—or both—had been doctored? The idea of Sabrina being harmed was unthinkable!

"We've already closed the casino, intending to go over the place with a fine-tooth comb," Caine said. "But I'm not holding out any hope."

Yet another unpalatable thought occurred to Burke. "I suppose my father will have to be notified."

"I can't see any way to keep him out of it," Caine agreed. "Not without endangering the rest of the family."

"Of course we cannot do that."

Although the sight chilled his blood, Burke looked down at the young woman once again, taking in the treacherous dark bruises on either side of her neck. Then, with remarkably steady hands, considering the circumstances, he pulled the black covering back over her unnaturally waxy face.

"I don't suppose she had any papers on her?"

"No."

He sighed heavily; his broad shoulders slumped. "When you learn her identity, I wish to be told immediately. It is my responsibility to extend my condolences to her family."

Understanding the Giraudeau's unwavering belief in family ties and royal obligations, Caine nodded. "I'll keep you informed of the investigation."

His expression was grave as he held out his hand toward the man who had become his brother-in-law two years ago and, more importantly, his friend. Burke shook hands with his sister's husband and felt a bond as strong as if Caine had been his own blood brother.

As he returned to the palace, Burke could not get the image of that poor dead waitress out of his mind.

The rented black sedan drove slowly by the police office as Burke emerged. The driver took careful notice of the guard walking beside the prince, just as he noted the men sitting in the two unmarked cars parked in front of the station.

His knuckles whitened as his hands tightened to a strangle grip on the steering wheel; the expression on his face suggested that he would love to put those strong fingers around the prince's neck.

He'd received a great deal of complaints concerning last night's failure. As well he should. It was, after all, what he deserved for relying on someone else—and a woman—to carry out such an important assignment. He was a professional. As such, he was well paid to perform. And he would. Soon.

The man's thin harsh lips curved in a cold smile as he anticipated the funds which would be waiting for him in the Geneva bank.

SABRINA COULDN'T FIGURE Burke out. There was absolutely no sign of the debonair, sophisticated prince whose company she'd enjoyed at the casino, nary a glimpse of the sexy, desirable man she'd nearly made love to in the limousine. Instead, although his behavior remained studiously polite, over the next three days he grew oddly distant. And surprisingly short-tempered.

Not that he wasn't an excellent host. Every afternoon, after his time trials, he would take Sabrina's family on a tour of his country. So far she'd seen the royal vineyards, the royal yacht harbor, the royal game reserve, the royal ski resort, and even the royal dairy herd, which Dixie, never without her guidebook, correctly identified as Swiss Brown cows. But for not a single second had he managed to find time to be alone with her.

Obviously Sabrina came to the conclusion on the afternoon before the race, Burke had changed his mind about wanting to make love to her. And, gentleman that he was, he didn't want to tell her outright that he no longer found her appealing.

Sabrina had known all along that the prince would regret his dalliance with a commoner. But she hadn't expected his change of heart to occur so soon. Neither had she expected it to hurt so badly.

Although in the beginning she'd assured herself that she wanted nothing at all to do with the playboy prince, during this past week in Montacroix, she'd definitely changed her mind.

Now, all she had to do was change his mind.

Claiming fatigue and a headache, she begged off on yet another afternoon sight-seeing trip. As soon as the limousine glided away from the palace, carrying her mother and sisters, along with Chantal, Caine and Burke, Sabrina shed her robe, revealing the flowered dress she was wearing beneath it.

Next she checked her purse, to make certain she had her credit cards. When Sabrina left the suite, she was smiling with anticipation. Twenty minutes later, she was in one of the pricey boutiques in the heart of the Alpine village, turning this way and that in front of the three-way mirror.

"It's *très chic, n'est-ce pas?* The ultrasophisticated saleswoman stood behind Sabrina, beaming her approval.

"It's very black," Sabrina agreed.

As she stared at her reflection, she was wondering if she'd done the right thing, putting herself into this woman's immaculately manicured hands. Then she remembered that the boutique had come highly recommended. Chantal had professed to purchasing several gowns here.

"Black is a perfect foil for your blond hair," Franqise pointed out.

That much was true. Still, Sabrina couldn't help feeling as if she were dressing for a funeral. Indeed, at least the dress she'd bought for her father's funeral had boasted gleaming pearl buttons down the front. "Perhaps a scarf," Sabrina mused, eyeing a bold red-and-gold silk scarf on the nearby glass counter.

"*Oh non, mademoiselle,*" the clerk said, clearly alarmed. Sabrina suspected that she would have been no less shocked if her American client had suggested torching her beloved boutique. "This dress is grand sculpture. Would one put a scarf on the Eiffel Tower? Or the Sphinx? Or even your own American Washington Monument?" She pursed her scarlet lips and shook her head. "I think not."

"Perhaps a chain?" Sabrina plucked a long pearl-and-gold chain from a display rack.

Franqise shook her blond head with obvious disapproval. "The magic of this gown is its starkness. It interests a man by making him imagine the woman underneath."

The flowing trapeze-style dress covered her from throat to wrists to ankles, providing nearly as effective camouflage as an Arab woman's voluminous cloak. Sabrina could only hope that Burke had a very vivid imagination.

"I don't know..." She hesitated, remembering the masculine approval that had shone in his eyes when he'd seen her in her brief gold slip dress.

"Mademoiselle asked for my opinion," the clerk said on a distinctly Gallic huff. "If you would prefer something else..."

"No." Reminding herself that she'd come here today to purchase a gown suitable for the upcoming coronation ball, something that would make her appear as sophisticated and cosmopolitan as Burke's usual women, Sabrina took a deep breath and said, "I'll take it."

As she handed over her American Express card, she could only hope that Burke's response would be worth the dress's outrageous price.

After arranging to have the dress sent to the palace, Sabrina went shopping for the appropriate shoes and bag. The shoes were black satin pumps, the bag was matching black satin with a simple gold clasp.

"Well," she muttered as she sat in a café and sipped an espresso and nibbled at a delicious chocolate-and-strawberry crème pastry, "at least I've got the wardrobe if I ever get cast as a grieving widow."

Although the somber hue and style of her purchases went against every feminine instinct she possessed, Sabrina had spent the past three days desperately trying to understand why Burke had seemingly lost interest.

Finally, the only answer she could come up with was that although he'd initially been attracted to her, he regrettably found her love of bright colors, flamboyant styles and down-home American attitude less than desirable.

And though she'd sworn never again to give up her independence for any other man, Sabrina rationalized her decision. After all, what was so important about a dress? What did it matter if she would have preferred something with a bit more pizzazz?

All right, Sabrina admitted, a *lot* more pizzazz. If wearing black allowed her to get what she wanted—and what she wanted was to see that dangerous, masculine gleam in the prince's dark eyes again—what was wrong with that?

"Nothing," she decided. "Nothing at all."

Lost in thought, Sabrina failed to notice that the sun

was beginning to set on the horizon. She also had no idea that several blocks away, a crowd was gathering. She sat a little longer, ordered a second cup of dark brew and, throwing caution to the winds—after all, her new dress would hide a multitude of guilty pounds—got another pastry.

Twenty minutes later, she paid her bill with a traveler's check, and walked out the door into chaos.

A crowd of approximately twenty-five people was marching down the street, loudly chanting antiroyalist slogans. At the head of the ruckus, a man wearing a black excutioner's hood was carrying a figure in effigy. The sign around its neck proclaimed it to be Prince Burke.

Although Burke had mentioned a small group of dissidents and had warned Sabrina's family against going outside the palace grounds without a male escort, actually seeing the protesters in action came as a surprise.

During all those excursions around the Montacroix countryside, she'd watched the prince's subjects respond to him with respect and genuine affection. It had also not escaped her notice that Burke returned their respect.

From what she'd been able to tell, he knew all his subjects' names, the names of their spouses and children. And more important, when he'd inquired after those absent members of various individuals' families, it had been readily apparent that he truly cared for, and about, his people.

Which was why she was so infuriated when one of the vocal protesters accused Burke of being a self-serving dictator.

"You're wrong!" she shouted, forging her way through the noisy throng. She was jostled, and almost fell, but with her anger came renewed strength and she pressed on.

"And even if your accusations had any truth to them, which they certainly don't, this is no way to address your grievances," she shouted at the hooded man who appeared to be the ringleader.

The man's response was a sarcastic laugh. Then, as Sabrina watched, he touched a torch to the gasoline-soaked figure. At the sight of the dummy bursting into flames, Sabrina's infamous Darling temper blew sky-high.

"What do you think you're doing?" She struck out at him. "Only a coward hides behind a mask!"

Sabrina's derogatory words had the effect of a match to kindling. The jeering crowd, given a focal point for their anger, turned on her. Women shoved her, men, their faces twisted with hatred, shouted in her face. One protester swung a heavy placard, hitting her on the shoulder and throwing her off balance.

Sabrina fell to her knees on the cobblestones and was in danger of being trampled when out of the crowd came a burly pair of arms to scoop her up and carry her through the swarming crowd to safety.

"Th-th-th-thank you," she gasped. "I don't know what I would have done if you hadn't..." Her voice trailed off as she realized exactly who her savior was. "It's you!"

Drew's worried eyes took in her smudged face, her tangled hair, her bruised shoulder. "Are you all right?" the man she'd come to know as a chauffeur inquired. He had a distinctly American accent she recognized as coming from her own state of Tennessee.

"Yes." She brushed at the dirt staining her flowered skirt. "Thanks to you."

"You shouldn't be wandering around alone. Prince

Burke won't like knowin' that you left the palace without an escort."

She wondered at the audacity of an employee to speak so disapprovingly to a guest, but still shaken and loath to admit it, she didn't call the chauffeur on his odd behavior.

The truth was that she'd been chafing against what she'd seen as an imperial order for the past three days. Ever since Burke had insisted that none of the female members of the household—guests included—leave the palace without a male escort.

Although he'd assured the women that it was only a precaution against possible problems with the insurrectionists, Sabrina had felt as if she'd been put under house arrest.

The idea of having some palace security guard hovering over her while she searched the village for an appropriate dress to dazzle Montacroix's dashing prince had been unpalatable.

Which was why she'd engaged in subterfuge in order to gain a few precious hours of freedom. But her rescuer was right about one thing, Sabrina reluctantly admitted—Burke was not going to be at all pleased when he discovered what she'd done.

"I don't suppose you and I could keep this little incident to ourselves?" she asked, fluttering her lashes in a way that Ariel's soap-opera vixen would have envied.

The giant shook his head. "Sorry." Reaching into a pocket he pulled out a familiar yellow bag. "How about some chocolate-covered peanuts? They're Princess Chantal's favorite."

As she accepted the proffered confection, Sabrina wondered how it was that a mere chauffeur was on such intimate acquaintance with the princess's snacking habits.

That nagging little question was forgotten as they returned to the palace and Sabrina tried to mentally prepare herself for Burke's upcoming lecture.

What Sabrina had no way of knowing was that Burke had learned of her escapade before the limousine had reached its destination at the Montacroix zoo. And although he was annoyed, he also empathized with the reasons for her defiance.

Sabrina Darling was not a woman accustomed to taking orders. Neither was she a woman who would adjust her behavior to suit any man. Even a prince. Accustomed to females fawning over him, more because of *what* he was, rather than *who* he was, Burke's interest was piqued even more by Sabrina's little rebellion.

His amusement disintegrated the moment he received the call that she'd been involved in some damnable demonstration. His irritation turned to concern when he'd learned that she'd been injured.

"Why weren't you with her?" he demanded of Drew, after he'd returned to the palace.

"I would've been a bit conspicuous in that hoity-toity little boutique," Drew countered calmly. Having provided protection for three U.S. presidents, he was not one to cower when faced with authoritative fury.

"You should not have let her linger in that café."

"Short of physically dragging her outside, I don't know what I could have done. Besides, I was keepin' an eye on her and everything would have been okay if she hadn't waded into the middle of those loud-mouthed idiots to defend your honor."

"What?" Burke dragged a hand through his dark hair. "She endangered herself on my account?"

"She reminded me of a mama bear protectin' her favorite cub."

"Come on, Burke," Caine said mildly. He'd taken his partner's place this afternoon. "Other than a few scrapes and bruises, Sabrina's fine. Don't you think you're making too much of this?"

Burke turned on his brother-in-law. "How would you feel if it had been Chantal who'd been injured?"

"I'd want to kill the bastard who laid a hand on her personally," Caine answered promptly. When he saw the identical look in Burke's eyes, he said, "So that's how it is."

"Yes."

Caine let out a long breath. "Talk about complications. How does she feel?"

"I don't know," Burke admitted with obvious reluctance.

He was a man accustomed to controlling his environment. Unfortunately these days he seemed to have little control over the most intimate aspect of his life.

"There will be time to discuss such matters after the coronation."

"Take it from a guy who's been there," Caine advised. "You ought to at least let her know how you feel."

How could he do that when he didn't entirely understand that himself? Burke wondered. "Right now, I'm going to ensure that Sabrina is resting all right," he said, his brusque tone announcing that the subject was closed.

"It's like looking in a mirror," Caine murmured to Drew after Burke had left the library. "Two years ago."

"The guy's got it real bad," his partner agreed. "This also puts a new twist on things. If anyone else figures out just how much the prince cares for Sabrina..."

He didn't finish the statement. There was no need.

"Oh! Your Highness." Monique dipped into a quick, deep curtsy when she opened the door to Burke's insistent rap. "I am afraid that mademoiselle is not seeing visitors."

"She'll see me." Burke entered the suite against the maid's faint protests and marched directly into Sabrina's bedroom.

For someone who wasn't up to visitors, Sabrina certainly had more than her share. She was lying on the bed, clad in a short, full-skirted flowered dress that made her resemble a garden in full bloom. She was surrounded by her mother and sisters. Chantal was hovering on one side of the canopied bed, Noel on the other.

"What did you think you were doing?"

At Burke's roar, conversation instantly ceased.

"You shouldn't be here, Burke," Chantal protested. "Sabrina has had a difficult experience. She needs her rest."

"As much as your protectiveness is undoubtedly appreciated, *chérie*, this is between Sabrina and me." He crossed his arms over his chest and glared down at Sabrina, who tried her best to glare back. "I want to talk to you."

She'd been an actress long enough to feign indifference when her heart was pounding. "So talk."

"Alone."

"Really, Burke," Noel chided, "your manners are atrocious."

"Madame Darling," Burke said, turning toward Dixie, "I apologize for my abrupt behavior, but I wish very much to speak to your daughter. In private."

Dixie beamed. "Of course, Your Highness. Come along girls," she said, ushering her other daughters from the bedroom, "we need to go over that third chorus of 'Honky Tonk Heaven' one more time. I thought the other day, during rehearsal, that you rushed that second line, Raven."

"You may be right, Mama," Raven agreed. She'd never rushed a line in her life. "See you later, Sabrina," she said, waggling her fingers at her sister as she left the suite with Dixie, Ariel and Noel. Only Chantal paused briefly.

"Be gentle with her, Burke," she murmured, her hand on his arm. "She's had a rough day."

With that little piece of advice, his sister left the room on a cloud of custom-blended perfume, leaving Sabrina and Burke alone.

Sabrina had expected Burke's anger. She'd even prepared herself for the type of icy disapproval her husband had so routinely used to punish her. But she'd never planned to see such honest distress in his dark gaze.

"How are you?" he asked on a low, deep voice that vibrated all the way to her bone marrow. "Really."

"Fine." She flashed him what was meant to be a reassuring smile. "Really."

Not waiting for an invitation, he ducked his head beneath the gauze canopy and sat beside her. "I was told you were injured." When he took in the sight of the bruises on her bare arm, Burke felt his temper flare.

As he touched the purple marks with an infinitely gentle fingertip, Sabrina watched the heat rise in his eyes and prayed such fury would never be directed her way.

"All I got were a few cuts and bruises." Her voice was little more than a whisper.

"But you fell." If Drew had not been there, she might have been trampled." The idea chilled Burke's blood.

"And scraped my knees. That's all. I had worse scrapes when I was a kid, running wild in the Tennessee woods."

Fighting down the urge to curse at the sight of her red, marred flesh, Burke retrieved the tube of ointment from a Queen Anne table beside the bed and squeezed a generous amount of the cream onto his finger.

"I would have liked to have known you then." His finger traced creamy patterns over first her left knee, and then her right.

Despite the effect his tender touch was having on her, Sabrina laughed. "You wouldn't have looked twice. I was too tall and too thin. The other kids used to call me Twiggy."

"You've filled out admirably." One hand cupped her leg, his thumb tantalizingly created circles on the sensitive back of her skinned knee. The other toyed with the golden waves that tumbled freely over her shoulders. "You have the most wonderful hair," he murmured, bringing it close to his face, inhaling the scent of her citrus shampoo. "It's like holding handfuls of sunshine."

If Sabrina had been frightened when she'd found herself in the middle of that loud, dangerous crowd, she was terrified by the way Burke, with just a look, a touch of the hand, could cause her to wish for the impossible.

Youthful dreams she'd worked so hard to put behind her returned, full-blown and enticing, like sweet, fragrant lilacs after a long harsh winter.

"When I was growing up in Nashville, I wore it in braids. I also had freckles and a mouth filled with railroad tracks."

"I like your freckles." He ran a fingertip over her cheekbones. "My sister Noel wore braces," Burke revealed. "She hated them. But now she has a beautiful smile."

His hand cupped the back of her neck and his eyes met hers. "Such orthodontia obviously worked just as well for you."

This had to stop. Now. Before she forgot where they were. Another moment of this sweet torment and she would be pulling him down on the bed beside her. Knowing that her mother and sisters were on the other side of that door, she tried again to dispel the sensual web settling over them.

"Burke." His name came out as a soft exclamation as his fingertip circled her lips. "Please."

Seeming entranced with the shape and texture of her lips, he ignored her whispered plea. "I have been thinking about you, Sabrina Darling," Burke murmured. "Night and day, thoughts of you fill my mind."

Sabrina didn't think it prudent to admit that he certainly wasn't alone there. "I wouldn't have thought I was your type."

He chuckled. "Neither would I. And I would have been wrong." Tangling her hair in his hands, he dipped his head and gave her a kiss so sweet it nearly brought tears to her eyes.

Sweet. She was so infinitely sweet. As his tongue slipped past her parted lips and was welcomed into the warmth of her mouth, he heard her soft, murmured approval, and felt a swelling of emotion stronger than anything he'd ever known.

Other women had made him want. Other women had made him ache. But no other woman had ever made him experience this emotional and spiritual need. She was like no woman he'd ever met. And Burke knew that if he searched the world over, he would never find anyone like her. Which was why he decided against stripping that flowered dress from her lissome body and burying himself in her soft welcoming warmth.

Burke still wasn't sure what he was feeling toward this woman. But he knew that whatever was happening between them, she deserved more than a quick, furtive tumble in the sheets.

He'd tried to keep his distance since that night in the limousine. He'd tried to give them both time to adjust to these unsettling emotions. He'd also been going crazy, hungering for a taste of Sabrina Darling's sweet lips.

Breaking the heated contact, he clasped her head between his hands and stared down at her lovely, flushed face. His breath was ragged. As was hers. "You need your rest."

Loath to sever the silken bonds of pleasure, she ran her palms down his back, reveling in the feel of muscle and sinew. "I told you, I'm fine."

"Oh, you are a great deal more than fine, Sabrina Darling." Still looking directly into her eyes, he grazed the tip of her breast with a fingertip, pleased when he felt it ripen beneath his touch.

A shudder of emotion rippled through her. She envisioned his dark head nestled between the thrust of her swelling breasts, imagined the feel of his lips on her burning flesh, fantasized him taking her tingling nipple between his strong white teeth.

She was trembling from his touch. Burke watched the myriad emotions in her eyes, each more erotic than the last, and knew that he'd *never* wanted a woman so badly.

Which was why to take her now, when she was still

shaken and vulnerable from this afternoon's incident, would be unconscionable.

It was out of sheer willpower that he released her and pushed himself to his feet.

Still caught up in her sensual fantasy, Sabrina stared up at him, uncomprehendingly.

"I seem to have acquired a bad habit of choosing the worst possible time and place to make love to you."

He ran the pad of his thumb along her bruised cheek and frowned again as he thought how badly she could have been harmed. On his account.

"Rest well, *ma chère*. Tomorrow, after I have won the race, we shall celebrate in style."

"You sound awfully confident," she complained, even as she secretly admitted that his boast, which would have seemed like arrogance from any other man, suited Burke perfectly.

"About the race, I am confident." He lifted her hand and brushed his lips across her knuckles. "About the celebration, I am hopeful."

With that he was gone. Leaving Sabrina wanting. And wondering how she was going to get through the next twenty-four hours.

8

THE COURSE for the Grand Prix de Montacroix curved past the Giraudeau palace, beyond the stables, around the north end of the lake, past the cathedral and the casino, before looping around, through a five-hundred-year-old stone tunnel cut into the Montacroix Alps, into a series of three hairpin turns, through the part of town dedicated to commerce, with its banks and stock exchange, finally returning again to the palace.

The assembled drivers—the very best in the world—would make that circuit fifty-six times before one of them would speed into the record books.

And all along the treacherously curving route, fans would congregate. Some would actually watch the racing, keeping track of the lap times, but most would come to socialize. Because congeniality and ambience were what made Montacroix the place to be—and to be seen—during Grand Prix week.

As Burke went over the prerace check with his crew, his mind—which never wandered prior to a race—kept drifting back to Sabrina. He pulled on his fireproof gloves, climbed into the cockpit, and took his earned position at the post for the pace lap. As he passed the palace, it was all Burke could do not to look up at the balcony in order to search her out.

Sabrina had never been more nervous in her life. Unable to stay still, she paced back and forth along the balcony, until Dixie complained about her blocking everyone's view.

"You're actin' like a long-tailed cat in a roomful of rocking chairs," her stepmother complained.

Which was, Sabrina thought, exactly how she felt. Her heart was in her throat, and her stomach felt as if it had taken off on a roller coaster ride, leaving her behind. She didn't want to watch, in case the unthinkable happened. For that same reason, she couldn't take her eyes off the track.

She kept her binoculars focused on Burke's red car. It was sleek and dangerous looking, resembling a manned cruise missile.

From the beginning, he lapped more quickly than the others, repeatedly setting the fastest lap and never giving up. If her interest hadn't been so intently personal, Sabrina knew that she would have found his daring a thrill to watch.

Right in front of the palace, a Porsche, driven by an American, came too close and brushed wheels with a black Lotus driven by the son of an Italian industrialist. The Italian braked, causing a third car coming up behind the pair to have nowhere to go but over the back of the Lotus.

Complete chaos ensued. A fourth car screeched to a grinding halt just short of the third, while a fifth careened into them both just as Burke came out of the tunnel into the turn. Jessica cried out, the regent cursed, and Sabrina held her breath as Burke attempted to get around the outside of the wrecked cars, spun one-hundred-eighty degrees, backed up, turned around and managed to push on. Behind him, the rest of the pack staggered by, more and more strung out.

"I knew he could do it," Eduard insisted on a voice that was far shakier than his usual strong baritone. "Do you remember when I avoided a similar crash in Monte Carlo, my dear?"

"I could hardly forget it," Jessica said dryly. "I had nightmares about you burning up in that car for months afterward."

"It could not have happened," Eduard insisted. "I was an expert driver. And our son inherited my skills."

As she watched Burke speed through the narrow streets, Sabrina wished she could feel as confident as Prince Eduard sounded.

THE MAN, dressed in an Italian pin-striped navy suit left the office of the Giraudeau Bank, headed down the fifth-floor hallway to the rest rooms. Once inside the stall, he opened his padded alligator briefcase and took out the disassembled pieces of the automatic rifle, putting them together with a deft skill that bespoke years of experience.

Outside the gray stone bank building, the deafening roar of the engines was making work impossible, which was why the employees had given up for the day and gathered atop the roof to watch the race. Rather than finding it a distraction, the man welcomed the noise; it would mask the sound of the gunshot. If all went as planned, it would appear as if the prince merely lost control of his car. With any luck, it would burn when it crashed; if not, at least the ensuing chaos would give him sufficient time to get out of the country before the authorities realized that their regent-to-be had died of a gunshot wound.

He took the key he'd stolen from the custodian's closet and locked the rest room. Then, using the stock of the rifle, he broke out the frosted glass in the rest room window. A window that conveniently offered an bird's-eye view of the racetrack.

Lifting the rifle to his eye, he squinted into the sun, adjusted the telescopic sight, then waited patiently for the red Ferrari to appear in the cross hairs.

BURKE HAD A HEALTHY LEAD when he pulled into the pit on the twenty-eighth lap to change tires. The pit crew excelled themselves, changing all four wheels in less than eight seconds.

As he roared out of the pit, Burke felt extremely confident. He was enjoying the beautiful weather and the challenging course, kissing the curbs on the hairpin turns, flying through the ultrafast corners with a master driver's precision. This Grand Prix was turning out to be a perfect prelude to his coronation.

But the race wasn't over yet. As Burke exited the tunnel on the forty-ninth lap, swooping out of the stone arch like a fighter jet on a strafing run, the driver who'd been in second place for the past ten laps tried to pass him on the inside. But he'd timed the move wrong, causing his car to be momentarily pinned against the stone wall. Then, completely out of control, it did a slow heart-stopping roll in midair over the top of Burke's speeding Ferrari.

The shrill screams of the engines muffled the screams of the spectators. Chantal, Dixie, Ariel and Raven covered their eyes and turned away, emotionally unable to cope with the horrific accident. Noel, Jessica, Eduard and Sabrina could not look away.

When the other car's tire creased Burke's red helmet, Sabrina felt the blood drain from her face. Her knees weakened and for the first time since the start of the race, she sank in one of the wrought-iron chairs flanking the balcony railing.

"He's all right!" Eduard shouted. "Look, he's continuing the race!" His chest was puffed out with paternal pride; his dark eyes, suspiciously moist, revealed his earlier fear. Beside him, Jessica sat, her fingers curled tightly around her husband's arm, silent tears streaming down her too pale cheeks. Sabrina felt similar tears on her own face and brushed them away with the back of her hands.

Burke blinked against the red veil obstructing his vision and pulled into the pit.

"That's it," his crew chief said. "You're done for."

"The hell I am," Burke retorted, yanking off his helmet. "I just need something to stop this damn bleeding." The blood, dark and deadly, was pouring from a two-inch gash on his forehead.

"You could have a concussion," Drew warned as one of the crew mopped away the blood with a towel and slapped a thick flesh-colored adhesive bandage against the prince's brow.

Another man, clad in a red Giraudeau team coverall, tossed the bloody helmet aside and handed Burke another one. Meanwhile, the remainder of the crew took advantage of the unscheduled stop to top off the gas tank and check the engine.

"You should be in the hospital," Caine, who'd joined his partner in the pit, said grimly.

"I'll have a doctor check me over after the race," Burke countered. Before anyone could object, he slammed the car back into gear and rejoined the race.

For a time it seemed as if the celebrated Grand Prix had turned into the Demolition Derby Sabrina remembered going to after Sonny's performance at a Tulsa, Oklahoma rodeo. Cars crashed into the heavy barricades and each other, leaving brightly colored metal parts scattered over the curving roadway. Tires shredded and engines blew apart, creating billowing clouds of black smoke that mingled with the odor of oil and exhaust on the soft summer air.

By the fiftieth lap, only four of the thirteen cars that had begun the race were still on the track. And despite two dangerous near misses, Burke was still in the lead.

She watched spellbound as the prince continued his smooth and exhilarating run, putting on the same polished performance to the finish, effectively annihilating the opposition.

And when the long race was finally over, she was laughing and hugging everyone on the balcony. As she felt herself being given a most unregal bear hug by the ebullient Prince Eduard, she felt as if she were one of the family.

BURKE SAT ON THE EDGE of the examining table, his bare legs dangling over the side, trying not to flinch as the doctor poured a stinging antiseptic over his wound. The pain was ripe and throbbing in his temple; his head swam.

"You must be one of the French loyalists who have been threatening to disrupt the ceremonies," he complained between clenched teeth. "Or else you're a sadist."

"There were rumors about the Marquis de Sade being my great-great-grandfather," the white-jacketed man answered blithely. "Of course the family has always chosen to ignore such stories." He dabbed at the cut with a sterilized swab. "My brother, however, is a dentist, which I suppose adds credence to such rumors."

He slid his glasses down his nose and studied the gash over the top of his tortoiseshell frames. "You are a very fortunate man."

"I've always been lucky," Burke agreed, deciding it

would sound like bragging to point out that his expert driving skills had contributed to him escaping what could have been a fatal collision.

"Still, not many men could survive two near crashes and a gunshot wound all in the same day."

"Gunshot wound?" Drew and Caine said in unison. They'd been waiting nearby. At the doctor's pronouncement, they snapped to immediate attention.

"*Oui*," the doctor answered. "As you can see, it is only a graze, but another millimeter to the right, Your Highness, and your father would have been planning a funeral rather than a coronation."

"It can't be a gunshot," Burke argued. "The wound is from Mario Francotti's front tire. I felt it brush my helmet." He turned to the two security agents. "You both saw it happen."

"We saw the accident," Caine agreed as he rubbed his jaw, concentrating on his memory of the rapid-fire sequence of events. "But sometimes, what we think we see isn't what really happened."

"This is *ridicule*." Burke shook his head, then wished he hadn't as a blinding light flashed behind his eyes. "What are the odds of getting shot and struck during a collision at the same time?"

Caine's expression was nearly as grim as it had been after Chantal's near-fatal experience in that Philadelphia fire. "I wouldn't want to calculate the odds. But I have a feeling that you were right on the money about being lucky. I'll bet that the reason that shot was off the mark was because the accident deflected the bullet."

"That would be," Burke said slowly, "a fantastic coincidence."

"Isn't it?" Caine agreed. He turned to Drew. "Why don't you see if you can retrieve the prince's helmet? And get some forensic guys busy calculating the direction of the shot, so we can start looking for our needle in a haystack."

"I'm on my way," Drew said. "I take it you're going back to the palace with the prince."

"Yeah." Caine had a sudden need to see Chantal. To make certain that his wife and child were safe. He turned to the doctor. "I'm going to have to insist that you keep this confidential."

The doctor nodded. *"Bien sûr."*

After arranging to have the bill sent to his accountant, Burke took the bottle of pain pills the doctor prescribed and returned to the palace with Caine.

Although it was more than two hours since he'd taken his victory lap, the narrow winding streets were still filled with merrymakers. Any one of the exuberant individuals could have been his attempted assassin, Burke mused as the gunmetal gray sedan made its way slowly through the crowds. The darkly tinted windows provided privacy, but for the first time in his life, he felt unreasonably exposed.

Someone had tried to kill him. Not once, but twice. And as disturbing as that idea might be, Burke knew, without a shadow of a doubt, that his would-be executioner would try again.

"Perhaps we should postpone the coronation," he murmured.

Caine shot him a sideways glance.

"Because of the women," Burke answered his brother-in-law's sharp, questioning look. "While I detest the idea of caving in to these terrorist demands, I cannot ignore the fact that Sabrina could have been killed that night at the casino. And now that he's failed again, this would-be assassin will be growing more frustrated. Who knows what he will do next?"

"It's your call." Caine's mild tone did not reveal his own feelings on the matter.

"Can you keep them safe? All of them?"

"We can sure as hell try."

Burke laughed, but the sound held no humor. "There are times, Caine, when I wish that you were a bit less honest."

Caine flexed his fingers on the steering wheel, attempting to ease some of the tension that had every tendon in his body feeling as if it were in a vise.

"If you want an ironclad guarantee, I can't give it to you. If you want my word that I will do my best to keep your family—and my pregnant wife—safe from these maniacs, you've got it."

As Burke considered his words soberly, he studied the faces of the crowd outside the window. Was it the older man in the black turtleneck? he wondered. The young man in tennis whites walking beside the stunning blonde dressed in a crocheted sweater and enticingly sexy suede shorts? Dammit, who was it who had managed to grasp so much control over his life?

"Your word has always been enough for me, Caine."

Caine nodded, his grim expression mirroring Burke's own.

It was agreed that they would keep the news of the bullet wound from the family for the time being. Eduard would of course have to know. But both Caine and Burke saw no reason in disturbing the women any more than they'd already been.

And although Burke knew that such a decision was blatantly chauvinistic, the part of him that had been brought up under the tenet of male ascendancy to the throne attempted to convince him that it was for the best. But later, as he'd deftly brushed aside his mother's and sister's concerns, Burke had suffered pangs of guilt that were nearly as painful as his throbbing head.

Although the rest of Montacroix continued to celebrate long into the night, Burke was not up to such revelry. Instead, after a brief family supper, he excused himself and went upstairs, where he downed two of the pain pills with a glass of water.

In minutes he was asleep.

SABRINA LAY ON HER BACK on the thick feather bed, staring up at the gauze of the high canopy. For the past three hours she'd been trying her best to fall asleep. For the past three hours she'd been failing. Miserably.

A virtual cavalcade of disconnected pictures kept tumbling through her mind: her first sight of Prince Burke, his face stained with oil and his eyes as hot as embers; the way he looked days later, when he'd approached her in the theater and stood so very close, and she'd seen their mutual attraction reflected in all those mirrors, blatantly obvious.

She remembered every devastating moment of that first shared kiss in front of Katia's portrait. She relived their entertaining time together at the casino and wondered why she'd even bothered to pretend that she hadn't wanted to go.

She knew that she'd never forget their stolen kisses in the back of the limousine, while the soft rain pattered on the roof. And most of all, Sabrina knew that if she lived to be one hundred, she would never—ever—forget the icy terror that had torn through her when she'd thought, for that long, suspended moment, that she was going to lose him. Before she even had him.

Sabrina had never been very assertive with men. Sonny, despite his own checkered past, or perhaps because of it, had been an incredibly strict father. None of his daughters had been permitted to date before their sixteenth birthdays. Telephone calls from boys had not been permitted, and Sonny Darling had always threatened that if any of his precious girls dared to call a boy, she would instantly lose telephone privileges.

By the time she was permitted to date, the word about Sonny's protectionist attitudes had gotten around and there wasn't a boy at Nashville Senior High School brave enough to ask Sabrina out. Sonny's reputation followed her to college, but although there had been a handful of young men intrepid enough to chance the singer's wrath by taking out his lovely daughter, Sabrina's absolute lack of dating skills left her too shy to accept their invitations.

Instead, Sabrina had immersed herself in the college drama department, where she found the stage a perfect—and safe—outlet for all her tumultuous emotions.

Her very first beau had been a fast-talking Yankee who swept her into his bed, onto his stage, and in front of a Connecticut justice of the peace before Sabrina had known what hit her.

When her marriage had broken up, friends had advised her to throw herself back into the social whirl. But feeling emotionally bruised, and uncomfortable with the New York fast life shared by so many of her contemporaries in the theater, once again Sabrina shunned the dating scene. Indeed, with the exception of a few platonic dinners with actors she worked with, evenings were spent in her apartment, studying lines and watching old movies on the Arts and Entertainment cable channel.

And now, as she tossed and turned, chasing the illusive solitude of sleep, Sabrina realized that her sex life resembled that of a cloistered nun. Even in her marriage, true passion had eluded her. From the night he'd taken her virginity, after they'd shared two bottles of champagne at the famed Rainbow Room, overlooking the dazzling lights of Manhattan, Arthur had always been the one to instigate lovemaking. He liked to instruct her what he wanted her to do, just as he directed her on the stage. Dedicated actress that she was, Sabrina had tried her best to give a stellar performance.

A goal in which she'd apparently succeeded. Because when she'd angrily informed him that she'd never—in six years of marriage—experienced an orgasm, the unflappable Arthur Longstreet had appeared honestly shocked by such an unwelcome revelation.

So here she was, twenty-eight years old, suffering in a too-lonely bed when the man she wanted with every fiber of her being was just down the hall.

"No!" she whispered, rolling onto her stomach and pulling the snowy down pillow over her head. She couldn't do it. She didn't have the nerve.

But then she remembered how close Burke had come to dying today. And how close she'd come to losing an opportunity of a lifetime.

It wouldn't be anything but a one-night stand, a little voice in her mind piped up. At best, a brief affair. Because in four short days the prince would become regent and she and her sisters would leave Montacroix, continuing the tour.

It wouldn't be the fairy-tale ending she'd dreamed of as a child. Prince Burke was not going to ride up on his white charger and carry her off to his castle, where they'd live happily ever after.

But, dammit, Sabrina decided, throwing the pillow onto the floor, at least she'd have one night—one magical, fairy-tale night—to remember all the rest of her life.

Making her decision, she left the bed, slipped into her robe, took several deep breaths to calm her galloping nerves, then headed down the hall.

9

AFRAID THAT SOMEONE would hear her knocking on Burke's bedroom door, and even more afraid that she'd lose her nerve, Sabrina took another deep breath, briefly closed her eyes and then, before she could change her mind, turned the antique brass handle.

When the door squeaked, her heart jumped to her throat and she pictured hordes of royal guards descending on her. She quickly slipped inside, shutting the door behind her.

After her quick race down the hall, the bedroom, by contrast, seemed as dark as the inside of a cavern.

Gradually shadows became forms, and Sabrina was able to view Burke, lying naked on his back in a magnificent high bed. He'd thrown the sheet off during his sleep. The moonlight slanting through the high palatine windows outlined his sculpted, muscled chest under the sprinkle of dark curls.

His hips were lean, and although she knew it to be wrong, she couldn't resist looking at his sex, which appeared half aroused. Her heart took up an erratic beat and her blood warmed. She dragged her gaze down his legs, unsurprised to find them strong and muscled. His feet were long and narrow and beautifully arched.

Sabrina stood beside the bed for a long silent time, drinking in the sight of this man she'd been so instantly attracted to, despite her best intentions. The man she wanted. The man she loved.

Love. The word, which her rational mind had not allowed her to consider, bounced around in her head like a steel ball in a roulette wheel. But instead of terrifying her, Sabrina felt a certain welcome calm. She did love Burke. Enough not to ask him for what he could never give. She would have to settle for only this brief time together.

And given the choice, a few fleeting days of absolute happiness were far preferable to a lifetime of regrets.

A soft summer wind sighed in the branches of the ancient oak trees outside the window. Inside, there was only the soft, steady sound of Burke's breathing. And the wild staccato beat of Sabrina's heart, pounding in her ears.

She remembered how, during the family's celebratory dinner earlier this evening, he'd assured everyone that he was fine, that he'd only suffered a slight concussion. But his eyes had been laced with pain and he'd promised a clearly distraught Jessica that he would take the pain pills the doctor prescribed as soon as he retired.

What if the pills had put him in such a deep sleep she couldn't rouse him? Sabrina wondered now. Or worse yet, what if he awoke only to turn her down? The humiliation would be horrendous.

But leaving now, and never knowing, would be worse.

Sabrina untied the ribbon holding her robe closed. It landed in an emerald satin puddle at her bare feet. As she sat on the bed the mattress sighed; Burke murmured inarticulately, but did not wake up. A dark lock of hair had fallen over his forehead. When Sabrina hesitantly brushed at it, her tender touch drew a smile.

Emboldened, she trailed her hand down his cheek, then traced the outline of his mouth. Her hand continued down the strong column of his neck, across his broad shoulders. She pressed her palm against his chest, liking the strong, solid feel of it. Burke exhaled a long breath and covered her hand with his. But he did not wake up.

It was exhilarating, this freedom to watch him, to touch him, unobserved. It made her head light; desire sang its high sweet song in her veins. Sabrina felt dizzy. She felt warm. She felt wonderful.

With a forwardness that once would have shocked her, she pressed her lips against his chest. His flesh was warm and tasted so marvelously, mysteriously male. When she flicked her tongue against one of his dark nipples, Burke growled and thrust his hands into her flowing blond hair.

Burke was having the sweetest, sexiest dream. He was lying on a sun-warmed beach in Monte Carlo, or Cannes, perhaps, with Sabrina. For some inexplicable reason, the beach was deserted, save for them, giving them the freedom to touch and be touched. To love and be loved.

Her beautiful, slender hands were like gentle birds as they explored his heated flesh; her warm sulky lips created a deep ache inside him that went all the way to the bone. Then farther still.

Her hair draped over him, carrying the scent of gardenias and feeling like strands of exquisite silk against his skin. He pulled her down on top of him, pressed her body to his, and ran his hand down her smooth back.

A warm ocean breeze caressed their bodies, the ebb and flow of the tide echoed their lovers' sighs.

"Sabrina," he murmured against her throat, drinking in her sweet scent. *"Ma chérie."*

She moved fluidly against him, making the fires burn even higher. "Oh, Burke."

She whispered his name once. Then a second time. And, as her lips brushed against his, teasing, tantalizing, a third.

This time her soft voice parted the gauzy curtain of his dream. Burke opened his eyes and found himself looking directly into hers. They were wide and misty and shone with a woman's secret pleasure in the slanting silver moonlight.

"If you are a dream," he murmured, skimming his hand over the emerald column of her silk nightgown, "please, don't ever wake me."

Sabrina gave him a womanly smile that reminded him of how Eve must have greeted Adam when she'd arrived in his garden, with her flowing silk hair, creamy flesh and tempting, dangerous female allure. Then she kissed his cheek, roughened with a day's growth of beard.

"I seem to recall you saying that you save 'please' for the really important things."

Her words sank in, having the effect of a fire alarm. *"Mon Dieu,"* he said, his hands tangling tighter in her fragrant hair, "you are real."

Lowering her mouth back to his, Burke kissed her. The kiss, long and lingering and infinitely intoxicating, went on and on and on.

"Extraordinary," he murmured as he nudged the thin strap of her nightgown aside with his mouth and kissed her shoulder.

With only his clever hands and his wicked, wonderful lips, Sabrina felt like she was floating. "What?" she managed thickly, wondering when exactly she'd lost control of the situation. When she'd first sat down on the bed, she'd been the one to touch. To taste.

But now her head was swimming and her bones were melting and she had surrendered all control—all power—to him.

"You."

He rolled over onto his side, bringing Sabrina with him. His hands followed the outline of her soft curves while hers trailed along the more rigid lines of his body, the smoothness of taut skin over muscle. "You are absolutely extraordinary."

"So are you," she whispered. And it was true.

For a long drawn-out time they lay facing each other, exploring the differences in their bodies by touch, by taste, by smell.

Outside the leaded glass window, a pale white moon rose. Inside, passion built. Sabrina was straining against Burke, eagerly, desperately.

His lips found one of her nipples and he sucked, drawing fire. Drawing life. As he kissed her swollen breasts, the sensitive back of her knees, the cord at the inside of her thigh, drawing a soft cry of absolute pleasure, Burke realized that he'd been wanting this woman all his life. He'd been waiting for her. She was everything he'd ever dreamed of in a woman, more than he'd hoped for in a wife.

Wife. That singular word, which he'd successfully and deftly avoided all these years, seemed so perfectly matched to Sabrina Darling that it could have been coined with her in mind.

Even more than any of the innumerable European princesses his father had invited to the palace during these past months, Sabrina Darling was a woman born to wear flowing satins and silks and rich, disturbing scents.

And she was his. All his.

Rocked by an unexpected and riveting surge of possessiveness, Burke swore at the silk barrier between them. His long fingers curled around the lace bodice of the nightgown and ripped it ruthlessly to her waist. Sabrina did not protest. Rather, she moaned and wrapped her arms around him. Her mouth locked greedily to his, her hands clutched at him as if she feared falling off the edge of the world. Pleasure burst from her to him; desire flared.

She was hot and smooth and fragrant; the torn nightgown clung to her damp skin. His name burst from her lips on a husky, sensual cry as Burke's ravenous mouth found her breast. Caught up in a whirlwind of passion, Sabrina was unaware of the breathless, erotic demands she uttered.

Burke's hands, and then his mouth, burned a slow path across her breasts, down her body, over her stomach, to the inside of her thighs. When his fingers slowly circled their way through the golden nest of curls, prolonging each touch, Sabrina arched her hips, offering, welcoming.

"Exquisite," Burke murmured, brushing a fingertip over her quivering, moist flesh.

"Please." Taut with anticipation, Sabrina dug her fingers into the sheets. Passion shimmered in that single aching word.

Needing no further invitation, Burke touched his tongue to the rising, pulsing bud. Startled by the flare that shot through her, Sabrina gasped and jerked away.

Infinitely patient, Burke soothed her with soft, husky words, touching and kissing his way around the ultrasensitive flesh, assuring her that he would not do anything she did not want him to do.

"You tell me when you're ready, *chérie*," he murmured, his cheek nuzzling the soft triangle of hair, his warm breath feathering the gold curls. "I promise, I won't hurt you."

She saw the truth in his eyes. She felt the love in his voice. And as his hand caressed her hip, Sabrina did something she thought she'd never do again. She allowed herself to trust.

"No," she whispered. "You'd never hurt me."

Her trust was strangely more staggering than her obvious desire. More sobering. Burke vowed to be worthy of it.

"Let me know what you want."

Tremors coursed through her. "I think," she said, on something close to a sob, "I'd like you to do that again."

Sensing that she was not accustomed to putting her needs into words, Burke didn't question her further.

He flicked his tongue once more against the pink nub. Although she closed her eyes and her fingers dug into his shoulders, this time she did not move away.

Encouraged, he began to suck lightly, tasting the honey, the warmth. "Do you like this?"

Sabrina gasped as first one finger, then two slid into her. All the time his mouth did not cease its sweet sensual torment.

"Oh, yes." Her thighs were trembling, a slick sheen of perspiration beaded up on her burning flesh.

"How about this?" His voice vibrated against her most intimate place, and then she felt his caressing fingers replaced by his tongue.

"I...don't...know." The wicked, clever tongue was licking at her, probing her secrets, drawing her out. "Yes," she admitted breathlessly. "Please. Don't stop."

Burke had no intention of stopping. In truth, as his own body throbbed with unrequited, painful need, he didn't think he could. Sabrina was like no other woman he'd ever met. She was an intriguing blend of sensuality and innocence. In fact, if he hadn't known she'd been married, by her initially shy response to what should be a natural part of lovemaking, Burke would have suspected that she was a virgin. She was, he realized, an emotional virgin.

The idea that no other man had ever brought her to such heights was immensely gratifying. As her hips began to rotate in uninhibited demand against his mouth, and the soft, eager sound of a woman approaching climax escaped her parted lips, Burke felt a surge of what he recognized to be purely chauvinistic satisfaction.

Sabrina could hardly breathe. Desperate, she wanted to beg him to wait, to give her a moment. But she couldn't get the words out. All she could do was hold on for dear life as he took her higher and higher.

Wetness was pouring from her, hot and thick. Then, finally, blessedly, secrets hidden for a lifetime exploded, hurling her across time and space.

She was still trembling from the aftershocks when she felt him enter her, fill her.

Smiling, Burke touched his mouth to hers, giving her a taste of herself. Silent tears streamed wetly down her cheeks, sparkling in the muted light like trails of diamonds. Still smiling, Burke gently brushed a tear away with his finger.

And then, although she'd never believed it to be possible, before she'd even recovered, he was driving her up and up again.

Lost in a passion of their own making, Sabrina wrapped her arms around him, hung on tight and followed Burke into the mists.

SABRINA LOST TRACK of how many times they made love that night. The lingering touches, the kisses, all melded into one another, like a series of sensual dreams.

Hours later, they were lying entwined, a tangle of naked arms and legs, when she heard the sound of a cock crowing outside the palace window. A pale silvery light was banishing the midnight shadows.

"I have to leave," she whispered.

"Mmmph." He pulled her tighter against him and buried his mouth against her throat. "Why?"

"It's almost morning."

"So?" She was so sweet. So wonderful. And, he reminded himself for the umpteenth time this night, she was his.

"If anyone sees me leaving your room—"

"They won't be surprised." He ran his palm down her back, pleased by her answering tremor.

That was, unfortunately, all too true. "You don't understand," she said, pulling away from his hypnotizing caresses. She sat up against the hand-carved headboard, glanced around for the sheet to cover herself, then decided that it was a bit late for modesty.

She looked so enticing, with her hair tumbled artlessly over her bare shoulders, with the flush of lovemaking tingeing her cheeks, and her lips full and dark from a night of kisses. Looking at her, all warm and flushed, Burke felt a renewed surge of desire.

"I'm trying."

"Perhaps it would help your concentration if you looked at my face."

Guiltily he dragged his gaze from her creamy breasts. "Touché. But, you have to understand, *ma chérie*, if you present a man with such sweet temptation..." He shrugged with an elegant continental flair that reminded her again what different worlds they came from.

Sabrina shook off the unhappy thought, refusing to allow it to detract from the pleasure she was still experiencing from their lovemaking.

"So much of my life has been public," she murmured. "I'd prefer to keep our affair private." If she was the only one who knew, it would hurt less when it was over.

Burke didn't like her use of the word "affair," but not wanting to get into an argument over semantics, he decided that it was merely a difference in their languages. From the way she'd opened to him like a delicate flower bud beneath a loving sun, Burke knew that Sabrina understood they'd made a commitment to each other.

"While I hate the idea of you leaving my bed, I suppose I can understand your concern." He lifted her left hand to his mouth and kissed her fingertips, one by one. As his lips brushed against the knuckles of the third finger, Burke ran through a mental inventory of the Giraudeau royal jewels in an attempt to determine which of the many priceless rings to give her.

Diamonds were too ordinary, emeralds too obvious. Rubies were always nice, and would go well with that dress she'd been wearing the first night, but his world was filled with women who wore rubies and emeralds and sapphires. Burke wanted something different for Sabrina. Something that was as special as she was.

"Burke?" Sabrina glanced up at him curiously. He seemed a million miles away. "Is something wrong?"

"What could be wrong?" He bestowed one of his bone-melting smiles on her. "Here I am, alone in bed with the most enticing, exciting, passionate woman in the world, and—"

She put her palm against his smiling mouth. "Only with you."

For some reason, it seemed important that he understand that what they'd shared was different. Special. So that years from now, when he had a beautiful wife and a handsome son who looked like him, a son who would also inherit a kingdom, he might, from time to time, think back on the American actress who had loved him.

"I know." It had been too long since he'd tasted those luscious lips—five minutes at least. So he bent his head, intent on kissing her.

Sabrina pulled her head back. "Was I that bad?"

Her cheeks flamed. Not with passion, Burke considered, but embarrassment. "On the contrary, you were wonderful. *Magnifique.* You are the most passionate woman I've ever been with, Sabrina. You did, in truth, wear me out."

His words sent a glow of womanly pleasure through her. "I suppose you're proud of yourself."

"Immensely," Burke agreed. "As you should be proud of yourself. You are, *chérie*, a natural-born courtesan."

Not realizing that Sabrina considered this a passing affair, Burke could not know how badly that particular description stung.

"I have to leave. Now." She was out of his arms and out of the bed before Burke knew what had happened.

"Sabrina?"

"What?" She picked up the discarded nightgown, realized it was torn beyond redemption, and began looking for her robe. "Is something wrong?" Burke left the bed as well. Locating the robe on the floor, he handed it to her.

Unable to meet his concerned gaze, she turned her

back and shrugged into the robe. "What could possibly be wrong?" she asked on a falsely bright voice that only wavered slightly.

"I believe that's what I asked you."

"I'm just tired," she hedged. Her fingers had inexplicably turned to stone. "Damn."

"Here. Let me." Reaching out, he tied the satin ribbon. As she watched the movement of those deft fingers, Sabrina remembered how they'd felt on her body, and experienced an unwelcome surge of heat. "There."

He stood back, observed her carefully and wanted to believe that fatigue from a sleepless night was the only thing standing between them.

Burke didn't want Sabrina to leave. But he also knew, from the determined look in her eyes, that short of tying her to the bedposts, he could not keep her here with him.

"I'm sorry about your gown." He traced the rent with his finger. "I'll buy you a new one."

"That's not necessary."

His dark eyes narrowed. "I said, I shall purchase a replacement."

The power was back, in spades. As was the mantle of unquestionable authority. Sabrina welcomed it; it reminded her that she had struggled too hard for her independence to cede it to any man. Even a prince who could make her burn.

"Fine. Feel free to buy an entire storeful of nightgowns if that will make you happy."

She was angry. And unhappy. And Burke was damned if he could understand why.

Not wanting to end things on such an unpleasant note, he said, "Do you ride?"

The question came from left field. "Ride? You mean horses?"

"Exactly."

"Of course." She eyed him warily. "Sonny had a stable of thoroughbreds. We all grew up on horseback. Why?"

"I'd like you to go riding with me this morning. We could have a picnic. After you have a nap," he tacked on, deciding that things might go smoother if she was not so fatigued.

"I have rehearsals."

"I happen to know that my family has invited your family on a cruise of the lake today. I also know that they accepted."

"Well, then, since I'm going to be aboard the royal yacht, I'm afraid I'll have to decline your offer, Your Highness."

So they were back to that. Wondering what had happened to all those soft endearments she'd moaned in his ear all night, Burke fought down a surge of unwelcome temper.

"I'm certain my family will understand that you have accepted another invitation."

"They'll get the wrong idea."

She thought of Prince Eduard, and his demand that Burke marry and provide him with an heir. If he thought his son was involved with a commoner, he would be less than pleased. And if he knew he was sleeping with her, he'd undoubtedly hit the roof.

"On the contrary, I think they'd probably get the correct idea."

He approached her, looped his arms unthreateningly around her waist and, ignoring her warning glare, kissed her. A long, delicious kiss that left her shaken.

"Come riding with me, Sabrina," he murmured, his hand stroking her back in a way that was anything but soothing. "The coronation is only two days away. There won't be many chances for us to be alone."

He kissed her cheek. Her temple. Her neck. "How can you allow such a golden opportunity to slip away?"

The truth was, she couldn't. "I suppose, I have to eat lunch."

Burke didn't even try to conceal his pleasure. Or his masculine satisfaction. "I'll have the cook prepare a basket. Whatever you like. Caviar, pheasant, pâté, champagne—"

"And to think I used to be satisfied with hot dogs and potato salad," she said on a laugh, giving in as she'd known all along she would.

Burke was right. Their time together was slipping quickly away, like sands through the hourglass she'd seen in Prince Léon's armory. Sabrina knew that if she passed up a chance to spend a halcyon afternoon with the man she loved, she'd spend the rest of her life regretting it. He gave her one last mind-blinding kiss, then let her leave. Burke was unsurprised to find that he missed her the moment she was gone.

Immersed in her own tumultuous emotions—dazzling memories of Burke's lovemaking, anticipation of their tryst, dread of their inevitable parting—Sabrina failed to see the figure hidden in shadows, watching with avid interest as she slipped silently back into her own room.

"RACE YOU TO THE GROVE," Sabrina called back over her shoulder, spurring her mount into a gallop. Behind her she heard a gruff masculine curse, then the pounding of hooves on turf as they raced along a ridge. The crystal blue waters of the lake stretched away below, sunlight glistening like diamonds on its smooth surface.

Sabrina laughed, reveling in the feel of the cool breeze ruffling her hair, delighted by the pure synchrony of her body with the tall gray horse beneath her. She stayed low in the saddle, falling into the rhythm of the horse as she sent him plunging toward the stand of oak trees that marked the finish line.

She was almost there, victory was nearly in her grasp when the powerful jet black stallion charged by, its hooves throwing up clods of moist earth as it edged her out first by a nose, a head, then finally a full length.

"Next time I'll beat you," she vowed, pulling up her horse as she reached the grove of trees. "I swear I will."

Feeling more carefree than he had in months, Burke grinned unrepentantly down at her from astride the splendid, glistening black stallion.

Gone was the dazzling gypsy of that first night. Nor was there any hint of the sexy Apache dancer he'd witnessed during rehearsal. Today, clad in a crimson, snap-front shirt, tight black jeans and a flat black fringed hat, tilted at a jaunty angle, Sabrina reminded him of a South American gaucho. Burke realized that he'd come to look forward to seeing what appealing character Sabrina would assume each day.

"Why, Mademoiselle Darling, didn't your famous father ever teach you that it's bad manners for a lady to swear?"

"It's also bad manners for a man to use his superior strength to humiliate a woman."

She wasn't really humiliated; far from it. But a highly competitive person by nature, she was a little piqued that Burke had stolen the race from her at the last minute.

His expression immediately sobered, but the teasing smile remained in his warm, dark eyes. "I didn't mean to humiliate you," he said as he dismounted and came over to her side.

The feel of his strong fingers around her waist, as he lifted her down from the horse, warmed her skin. "Well, you did."

"I'm sorry." He moved so that his body was brushing against hers. "Whatever can I do to make it up to you, mademoiselle?"

Heat from his body was seeping into her own bloodstream. "Nothing," she pouted prettily, enjoying the game.

"Nothing?" His fingers and thumbs caressed her ribs with a tantalizingly tender touch.

"Not a thing," she insisted with a toss of her head.

"Are you so sure of that?" Lifting her hand to his lips, he pressed a kiss at the base of each long, slender finger. "There must be some small penance I could perform."

When his tongue drew a moist, warm circle at the center of her palm, Sabrina experienced a shock of pleasure so strong that her legs threatened to give way from underneath her.

"I really wanted to win," she complained breathlessly, wrapping her arms around his neck as much for support as in passion. Her head was buried in his shirt and she could hear the rapid beat of his heart beneath her cheek.

"Ah, but *ma chère*," he murmured, lacing his fingers through her hair to tilt her head back, "the day is not yet done."

The day had taken on a still and golden hue. "Does that mean that you'll race me again?"

His mouth curved into a slow, knowing smile. "It means," he said, briefly brushing his lips against hers, "that before this day is over, we will both be winners, Sabrina."

His words were spoken with the usual cocky self-assurance, but Sabrina could read the unspoken question in his eyes. After last night, she wondered why he felt the need to ask.

As he read the answer in her eyes, Burke felt an urge to lower her to the lush, flower dotted meadow. But always aware of his silent shadow, he resisted.

Next time, he vowed. *After the coronation. When all this dangerous talk of rebellion is over.*

"Come with me." He linked their fingers together and led her into the grove.

"Anywhere," Sabrina answered, meaning it.

Hidden amidst the trees, was a small cottage. Burke extracted a heavy iron key from the pocket of his fawn-colored jodhpurs and inserted the key into the ornately carved lock.

"This cottage originally belonged to the first royal gamekeeper," he said, pushing the heavy oaken door open. "We've added electricity, although it's been known to go out during thunderstorms. Since it's small enough to allow it to be heated by the fireplace, we haven't bothered with central heating. And although my father installed a telephone, Chantal took it out when she used the cottage as a studio for her painting. She claimed it was too much of an interruption."

"A telephone can be horribly intrusive," Sabrina murmured with a slow, sensual smile.

"Agreed." Unable to resist the lure of her satiny skin, he nuzzled her neck. "I've been racking my brains trying to think of someplace we could be alone. Someplace I could make love to you without danger of interruption."

Sabrina appreciated his thoughtfulness.

"It's perfect." The cottage was, indeed, both serene and private.

"I was afraid you might find it too rustic."

Since she loved him, Sabrina felt she owed it to Burke to be completely honest. "Actually, I think I prefer it to the gilt and glamour of the palace. As beautiful as your family's home is," she said quickly, not wanting to offend.

But instead of appearing offended, Burke laughed. "Now you sound like Noel. Every time my father turns around, my sister has come up with yet another scheme to, as he puts it, give away all our worldly goods."

"You sound as if you approve."

"As chairman of the Montacroix social services agency, it is my duty to help her do it," he said simply. "Traditionally the people of Montacroix have been taken care of from the cradle to the grave," he explained, alluding to the wealth of services provided by the privileged pocket principality.

As he talked, his hand pulled her shirt free of her

waistband. Her skin was warm and silken; he could feel the increased beat of her heart as his palm cupped her lace-covered breast.

"And while I agree with that idea in concept," Burke continued, struggling to keep his mind on their conversation, "I've also been trying to look at different ways of providing essential service."

"That's probably for the best," she agreed breathlessly as she moved against him in unmistakable feminine invitation.

He slipped his knee between her legs and ran his tongue in a hot wet swath down her arched neck. "We are becoming a global economy. And although my father steadfastly refuses to believe it, there are other places in the world besides Montacroix."

His knee, pressed against her aching warmth, was making her wet. Wanting to give him a bit of his own erotic torture, she pressed her palm against his hard male heat. "I doubt that your father would be thrilled to hear you talk this way."

The touch of her hand against his sex, the caress of her fingers, made Burke feel as if he were going to explode. "He considers it sheer heresy." His breath was rough and ragged and his hands, as they struggled with the pearlized snaps on her scarlet shirt, were far from steady.

From what she'd seen of Prince Eduard Giraudeau, Sabrina knew that his reputation for an iron will and blustering temper was well deserved. That his son and heir could disagree with him and still maintain a working relationship spoke highly of Burke's diplomatic skills.

"Yet you don't hesitate to press your views," she gasped as her shirt fluttered to the floor.

Beneath the shirt she was wearing a lace-and-satin

confection emblazoned with poppies. "I refuse to apologize for speaking the truth."

When he kissed her breasts, and her sweet, intoxicating, flowery scent played havoc with his senses, he felt the last of his self-control—that steely, reliable restraint he'd worn like a suit of armor for so many of his thirty-five years—ebb away.

When his hot lips captured her lace-clad nipple and tugged, Sabrina felt a tug between her thighs.

"Burke?" she said on a soft, breathless little sigh of pleasure.

His fingers deftly dispatched the bra's fastener, giving his mouth access to her fragrant, flushed skin. "What, *ma chérie?*"

The feel of his mouth against her bare flesh made Sabrina tremble. "I've decided to be gracious and forgive you for winning our race."

Her hands combed through his dark hair; her greedy, avid lips met his and clung. Outside the cottage, a hidden wood thrush sang.

Burke scooped her up into his arms and carried her across the room to the bed, covered in a gaily colored patchwork quilt.

As the perfect afternoon slowly ripened, that was the last either Sabrina or Burke said for a very long time....

IT HAD NOT ESCAPED Burke's attention that Sabrina and her sisters had a great many loyal fans. Her fame fit her well, he'd decided, after watching her sign autographs with a friendly, unaffected flair.

"The trick," she'd said when he'd mentioned her unpretentious attitude, "is never to make the mistake of believing your press. Because deep down inside, where it counts, I'll always be just a small-town girl from the hills of Tennessee."

Burke understood her words to be a warning, a vivid reminder of the vast differences in their social stratum. But her admonition fell on deaf ears. Because he was finding it increasingly difficult to remember all the reasons why the lovely American performer would not make a perfect princess for his beloved Montacroix. And more important, an exquisite wife and mother for his children.

He was pacing in the garden, considering how to broach the subject Sabrina seemed so determined to avoid, when he turned a corner in the maze and ran into his stepmother.

"I'm sorry." Burke bent down to retrieve the pink and white blossoms that had scattered over the narrow earthen pathway. "I'm afraid I wasn't watching where I was going."

Jessica smiled as she slipped the rosebuds in among the others nestled in the wicker basket she was carrying over her arm. "I assume your mind was on the lovely Sabrina?"

Burke answered her question with one of his own. "May I ask you something?"

"Of course."

"Do you remember when you first met my father?"

"I recall every detail of that day. The sky over Mykonos was a bright, cloudless Mediterranean blue. We'd been shooting all morning and I was out of sorts and tired of sitting on that hard, rough rock. While the cameraman worked out a new angle, my attention wandered and all of a sudden, I saw your father, standing on the beach. It sounds like a cliché from every movie I ever made, but our eyes met, and although I knew it was impossible, I could have sworn I heard thunder rumbling in the clear sky."

She laughed, a rich, musical sound that had entranced audiences for ten magical years. "Your father was no less affected. He told me that evening that he felt as if he'd been struck by lightning."

Burke shoved his hands into his back pockets and glared out at the diamond-bright waters of Lake Losange. "I know the feeling."

"Of course you do," Jessica agreed. "No one in the dining room could have missed your initial response to Ms. Darling."

He frowned at the idea that his emotions had been so blatantly obvious. Burke had always prided himself on keeping his inner feelings to himself. A future regent must always appear self-assured and confident, his father had told him time and time again. He must not allow his subjects to know that he suffers the same doubts and fears as they. Such apparent weakness endangers not only the monarchy, but the entire country.

This was the tenet upon which Prince Burke Giraudeau de Montacroix had been reared. And he'd succeeded, admirably. Until a dazzling enchantress had burst into his life, turning everything—including his heart—upside down.

"May I ask you another question?"

Jessica reached out with maternal concern and brushed a lock of dark hair from his furrowed brow. *"Certainement."*

"How did you feel? When father told you that he loved you?"

"Terrified," Jessica answered promptly.

It was not the answer he'd been expecting. Or hoping for. "But why?"

"Our lives were so different." Jessica waved a graceful hand around the garden maze, her gesture meaning to encompass not only the palace grounds, but the entire kingdom. "Your father was a prince who grew up in a palace. And although I'd starred as a princess in an MGM musical, I honestly didn't believe that I could carry out that role in real life."

"But you were famous," Burke protested. "Your name was linked with the most influential, powerful men in both Europe and America. You were a Hollywood movie star, back when such people were viewed as the most glamorous individuals in the entire world."

Indeed, looking at her now, in her gauzy white dress and wide-brimmed straw hat, with the wicker basket overflowing with roses on her arm, she could have been that lovely young actress who'd charmed so many men on so many continents.

"That was an image carefully cultivated by my studio," Jessica corrected mildly. "The truth was, I'd never stopped thinking of myself as little Jessie Thorne, that barefoot hillbilly girl who grew up in a hollow in West Virginia's coal mining country."

"Sabrina said she never believed her press," Burke murmured, realizing exactly how much this woman he'd come to think of as his mother and the woman he wanted for his wife had in common.

"Sabrina Darling is not only beautiful, she's talented, intelligent, and obviously has her feet well planted on the ground."

"She doesn't think she's princess material."

Jessica reached up and patted his taut cheek. "Then you'll just have to think of something to change her mind, won't you?"

And he would, Burke vowed. After the coronation.

THE MOOD ON THE DAY of the precoronation public celebration was definitely festive. This afternoon's performance would be held outdoors in order to accommodate the vast crowd. A stage, along with the towering screen that was so essential to the Darling's performance, had been set up at one end of the parade grounds; across the expanse of dark green grass, vendors from all over the country had set up gaily decorated stalls selling food and drink and hand-crafted, one-of-a-kind items. Members of a Russian circus, dressed in native cossack uniforms, performed daring stunts on horseback, while sad-faced clowns did pratfalls and pretended to throw buckets of water onto the crowd impatiently waiting in the tiered grandstand for the three American performers' arrival.

Raven, Ariel and Sabrina ran onto the stage to a thundering round of expectant and appreciative applause. And they did not disappoint. As he watched their hour-long performance, Burke, who'd seen them rehearse, found himself absolutely spellbound.

What Drew had said was true, Burke decided. Ariel, clad in a shimmering white gown, was the most conventionally beautiful of the three sisters, and Raven, with her throaty contralto, had obviously inherited Sonny Darling's talented voice.

But it was Sabrina who possessed the late country singer's ability to capture an audience and sell a song. When she stood in front of the enormous screen, facing the larger-than-life image of her father, and sang a soulful ballad about two star-crossed lovers finally united in honky-tonk heaven, the more emotional members of the audience began to sob quietly. Indeed, Burke felt a suspicious moisture burning at the back of his own lids.

And then, the tempo changed and Sabrina was strutting across that vast stage on her long lissome legs, belting out an up-tempo rockabilly tune of her father's that had topped the country charts for an unprecedented twenty-six consecutive weeks.

Burke joined the audience in a standing ovation. And by the end of their third encore, he vowed to do whatever it took to convince Sabrina to remain here in Montacroix. With him.

Her sisters had joined the public party. At Chantal's request, Sabrina had remained behind in the tent that had been erected to serve as a dressing room.

"Although I hadn't thought it possible," Chantal said with a smile, "you and your sisters actually managed to top your Washington performance."

Sabrina did not believe the princess had asked to speak to her alone in order to compliment her on her performance. "We received a lot of energy from the crowd. That always helps."

"I would imagine it would," Chantal agreed. For the first time since Sabrina had met the princess, she seemed decidedly uneasy. "Sabrina, I want you to understand that it is not my habit to interfere in the lives of my brother or sister. However—"

Here it comes, Sabrina thought when Chantal paused.

"I love my brother very much."

When Sabrina didn't answer, Chantal took a deep breath and probed a little deeper. "I believe you do, too."

Unnerved by feelings that she'd tried desperately not to feel, let alone put into words, Sabrina sat at the dressing table, plucked a handful of tissues from a nearby box and began to remove her heavy stage makeup.

A pregnant silence swirled around them. "All right, I do," she said on a soft sigh of surrender.

"*Bon.*" Chantal nodded her glossy dark head. Her dark eyes, so like her brother's, met Sabrina's gaze in the mirror. "But why does this make you so unhappy?"

Sabrina's hands trembled as she spread the fragrant white cream over her face. "Because the entire situation is impossible."

"But why?"

"Our lives are light-years apart," Sabrina said on a burst of feeling.

Chantal's answering sigh was audible. "Caine felt the same way, in the beginning. But finally he came to understand that the love we had for each other was stronger than any differences in our bank accounts or the size of our homes."

"No offense intended, Chantal," Sabrina said, scrubbing viciously at her cheeks, "but it's a whole lot easier for you and your husband. You moved to Washington. You chose to live your husband's life. Caine doesn't have to live here in Montacroix, being smothered in that museum you and your family call a home."

Sabrina shook her head as she heard how meanspirited her words sounded. "I'm sorry. I didn't mean that about your home. It's truly lovely."

In truth, during her time in the palace, Sabrina had been surprised to find herself actually growing accustomed to being surrounded by so many treasures. She could even walk across a room now without worrying about knocking a priceless vase off its marble pedestal. Such confidence was, she supposed, in its own way, progress.

Chantal lifted a dark brow. "You believe my brother would smother you?" She graciously did not, Sabrina noticed, respond to the impolite dig about her family's home.

"No. I think Burke would try his best to make me

feel comfortable. But it wouldn't work. Besides, it's a moot point. Because your brother hasn't proposed."

"He will," Chantal predicted.

"It wouldn't work," Sabrina insisted, wishing she sounded more vehement.

"Because of these so-called differences in your lives?"

"Yes." Sabrina tossed the soiled tissues into the wastebasket. "Stories about handsome princes rescuing fair damsels and carrying them off to their castles make nifty fairy tales, Chantal. But they don't play in real life."

"Giraudeau men have a history of falling in love and marrying exciting, independent women," Chantal argued, displaying a deep-seated tenacity that was an obvious genetic gift from Prince Eduard.

"Grandfather Phillipe married Katia, the gypsy, and my father wed an American film star. So, you see—" she shrugged her silk-clad shoulders "—it's only natural that Burke would chose an actress as his bride."

After receiving Sabrina's reluctant promise that she would at least give Burke the opportunity to state his own case before making up her mind, Chantal left.

Outside the gaily striped tent, there was the sound of music and laughter. Inside, there was only a deep, lonely silence.

11

DESPITE CHANTAL'S optimistic words, Sabrina was not convinced. Because even if Burke did propose, she didn't believe she'd dare accept. She couldn't see herself being married to a man responsible for the welfare of an entire nation. Burke needed a serene, serious wife with proper diplomatic and social graces. One his people could respect and admire.

Late that night, after the charity fund-raising concert, Sabrina stood at her bedroom window and stared out over the moon-gilded lake.

Her thoughts were in a turmoil, scattering here and there like leaves tossed around by hurricane-force winds. It was late. The rest of the household had gone to bed, but Sabrina couldn't sleep.

More than ever, she understood Maggie's tumultuous passion. Because tonight Sabrina was the one feeling like a cat on a hot tin roof.

So engrossed was she in her stirred-up emotions, she failed to hear the door to the adjoining living room suite open.

"*Bon*," the deep, wonderfully familiar voice murmured. "I was hoping you'd still be awake."

Desire ripped through Burke at the sight of Sabrina, standing in the moonlight, dressed in a lace-trimmed silk teddy that was as scarlet as sin and made her look as if her legs went all the way to her neck.

Rather than the silk dressing gown she would have

expected a prince to wear—the type David Niven wore in all those late, late movies—Burke was clad in a pair of cream linen trousers and a white sweatshirt embossed with the Oxford university emblem. His feet were bare.

"It's leftover stage energy," she fibbed. "I can never sleep after a performance."

"I am usually the same way after a race," he acknowledged, adding to his growing list of things he and Sabrina had in common. "You were wonderful."

The smoldering warmth in his gaze threatened to scorch her skin. "Thank you."

He crossed the room to stand in front of her. "I couldn't keep my eyes off you." With his hands splayed on her waist, he drew her forward. "I knew that you were talented." He touched his mouth against hers, capturing her soft sigh. "Even so, I was stunned by your beauty." His tongue outlined her lips, creating a dizzying trail of sparks. "And your energy, and—"

"Burke," Sabrina interrupted on a desperate moan. "Would you do me a favor?"

His hand caressed her arched neck; his thumb rubbed a slow, lazy circle against her wild pulse beat. "Whatever you wish."

"I wish you'd please shut up and kiss me." She ran her hands down his arms, slipped them beneath his sweatshirt and pressed her palms against his chest. "Your Highness."

Her fingers were playing in the dark pelt of hair covering his torso, making his flesh burn. "Anything to oblige a lady," Burke rasped, his voice rough and raw. He twisted his hands in her hair and tilted her head back, capturing her mouth in a hot, ravenous kiss.

His rampant tongue swept the dark moist vault of her mouth, seeking out her tongue, engaging it in an erotic ballet that was both imitation and prelude of the lovemaking yet to come. Tumbling headlong into the kiss, Sabrina moaned softly and wrapped her arms around him, tightly, pressing her trembling body against his in unspoken yet undeniable need.

All the differences between them disintegrated, blown away by the rising, heated winds of desire.

"Do you have any idea," Burke gasped when they finally came up for air, "how much I want you?"

"Yes." Breathless, nearly delirious, Sabrina buried her lips in the hot flesh of his throat. "Nearly as much as I want you."

Her absolute honesty was one of the many reasons he'd fallen in love with her. Tugging gently on her hair, he coaxed her liquid gaze back to his. "I'm all yours."

With that simple statement, Burke was offering Sabrina more than his body. Or even his love. He was, quite literally, offering her all the days, and nights, of his life.

Integrity warred with desire. Honesty battled passion. Sabrina knew that she should insist that all they could ever have was this mystical, magical time together. She realized, with the brilliant clarity of shared emotion, that Chantal had been right; Burke wanted her to remain in Montacroix with him. She also knew that to make love with him tonight would be implying a promise she could not keep.

But, dear heaven, she was terrified that if she told the truth, explained that she could not stay, Burke's ego might be so wounded that he would never make love to her again.

And that was something Sabrina was not prepared to risk.

So, turning down the volume on that little voice of

conscience, she gave him a slow, warm, womanly smile.

"All mine?" she challenged teasingly. "To do whatever I want?"

He released the silken tangle of her hair and held his hands out to his sides. "You're free to have your wicked way with me."

"In that case…"

Sabrina took hold of the bottom of his sweatshirt and worked it up over his rigid, flat stomach, over the ebony pelt of chest hair, going up on her toes to pull it over his head. His dark hair fell back into place, several thick strands tumbling over his forehead, making him look sexily mussed.

"That's better." Drawn by a torso that could have been the model for any of the palace's Renaissance sculptures, she pressed her mouth against his chest, delighting in the tingling feel of his springy jet hair against her lips.

"Much better," Burke agreed, drawing in a quick, sharp breath when her tongue grazed a nipple. Heat rushed over his bare skin. His trousers were growing tighter and more uncomfortable by the minute.

As if reading his mind, she knelt and dipped her tongue sensually into his navel, rewarded when she heard his ragged groan. Encouraged, and feeling wickedly, atypically bold, she moved her fingers to his fly and unfastened the first button.

Hunger had claws. Burke leaned back against the mahogany dresser and closed his eyes. "Oh yes," he murmured. "That's better yet."

She pressed her palm against his rigid erection, dizzy with feminine power. Power she understood he'd willingly ceded to her. When her mouth replaced her hand, she felt his body stir violently beneath the rough linen.

Slowly she released each button, one at a time, each time treating him to a warm embrace of her lips.

"Gracious." From her kneeling position on the Aubusson carpet, she looked up at him, her eyes dancing with merriment. His skimpy silk briefs were both a surprise and a delight.

"I received several pairs as a gift from a Paris designer several years ago and haven't bothered to wear them," Burke revealed, a bit uncomfortably, Sabrina thought. "After our afternoon in the cottage, they seemed appropriate."

"Oh?"

"They remind me of how your silken skin feels against mine."

"Oh." The sensual vision caused moisture to gather between her thighs. She trailed her fingers along the low-slung waistband, pleased by the animal growl that emanated from deep in his throat.

And then, with a boldness that would have appalled her even a day ago, she pressed her open mouth against the ebony silk, reveling in the strong male body that stirred so violently at her intimate caress.

"Sabrina," Burke moaned, "if you want me to beg—"

"No." Her hands embraced the firm flesh of his inner thighs. "I'd never ask you to do that."

Answering his unspoken plea, she pulled the silk briefs down the strong dark columns of his legs. He stepped out of them and reached for her, but she shook her head. Sensuality was pumping through her veins like a narcotic, more powerful than the adrenaline she'd felt earlier during her performance. Sabrina felt wonderfully, exuberantly, alive.

She nuzzled her face in the dark hair surrounding his rampant sex, loving the springy feel, the warmth, the musty taste. Her fingers encircled his length, stroking him lovingly, fascinated by the silky smoothness.

"My God, Sabrina!" Burke knotted his hands in her hair once more, wanting her to stop. Wanting her never to stop. She was killing him slowly with her touch. With her lips. With her warm and sensual tongue.

When that tongue made a long wet swath the entire length of his aching arousal, circling the dewy tip with all the sensual instincts of a natural-born courtesan, Burke's tautly held control snapped.

Foregoing what he'd always proudly considered a suave approach to lovemaking, he half carried, half dragged her to the bed, tossing her unceremoniously onto the mattress.

"If you continue to play so recklessly with fire, Sabrina, my love, you will burn down my family's two-hundred-year-old home."

She'd landed spread-eagle on her back, her long legs splayed, the lace-edged teddy riding high on her hips. Her hair was spread out on the linen pillowcase like an angel's gilded halo. But as she looked up at him, all wide sensual eyes and luscious wet lips, she looked anything but angelic.

When he lay down beside her, Sabrina rolled over and knelt above him. "When I was a just a little girl, back home in Tennessee," she said breathlessly, "I used to go to summer camp." Her mouth retraced that burning path down his throat, over his chest and stomach. "Want to know what my favorite part was?"

Hunger. He was delirious with it. Passion. He was mindless from it. Blood pounded in his head, his heart, his aching loins.

"Horseback riding?" Burke managed to croak.

"The camp fire." Her searching lips reclaimed him, driving him to the very brink of madness. Her voice, usually modulated from voice lessons, had slipped back into her soft Tennessee roots. "I have always just loved buildin' fires."

"No wonder." His desperate fingers reached between their bodies to unfasten the snaps that were guarding her feminine secrets. "Since you're so very, very good at it." Roughly pushing the crimson silk aside, he pulled her astride him.

Even as Burke arched his hips off the bed, Sabrina was moving downward to meet him. As he finally claimed possession of her slick body, she claimed his.

Their lips met with strangled cries of shared pleasure. And then they began to move in unison, faster and harder, higher and higher, until they took the final glorious leap into oblivion together.

THE CORONATION was scheduled for the following evening. Sabrina was disappointed, but not surprised when Burke's duties kept him at the cathedral all day.

She'd be leaving with Dixie and her sisters tomorrow morning. And although there was still the ball to attend, she doubted if she and Burke would be able to steal much more private time together.

"At least, we'll always have Montacroix," she murmured as she finished dressing for the coronation ceremony. She was in her most conservative attire—an electric blue silk suit adorned with shiny gold buttons and a matching hat that dipped low over one blond brow.

"What did you say?" Ariel asked, entering Sabrina's room in search of her misplaced gloves. Her sister's dress was emerald green, a brilliant foil for her red hair. Raven had chosen an ivory raw-silk suit, while Dixie was in basic black.

"Nothing." Sabrina spotted the kid gloves on a nearby table, tossed them to her sister, gave herself one last judicious perusal in the beveled floor-length mirror, then said, "Ready?" Her patently false smile was bright, belying the fact that her heart was breaking.

The coronation possessed all the pomp and circumstance Sabrina would have expected from such an important, solemn occasion. It also effectively drove home exactly how different her world was from Burke's.

The most solemn event of her life had been her father's funeral. And even there, Sonny's long-time friends and fellow performers had somehow managed to bring a festive air to the proceedings by telling side-splitting tales about Sonny's antics during his early days in Nashville and singing the songs he'd made famous.

Needless to say, there were no bawdy tales told at this event. Nor would any country songs be heard inside these august stone walls. Chantal had been right about the chamber music. She'd failed to mention the Bach.

The invited audience was, indeed, prestigious. Members of other royal families—the men handsome in dark suits, the women resplendent in formal dress and sparkling tiaras—shared the front pews with various heads of state. In the pew in front of her, on the aisle, Sabrina recognized the vice president and his wife, along with two former presidents.

Marble statues of former rulers, commissioned by Burke's great-grandfather Léon, lined the walls, looking down on those gathered for today's ceremony.

While she waited for Burke's entrance—which

Chantal had told her would be in the same royal coach that Napoleon had ridden in when he'd come to the cathedral to crown the first regent of Montacroix—Sabrina studied the magnificent building, taking in the graceful Norman columns, the towering windows whose stained glass caught the afternoon sun, scattering the light so that each colorful piece glowed.

At the stroke of six o'clock, the hammered-copper doors at the back of the cathedral swung open. The choir, on cue, began the processional.

The bishop of Montacroix, clad in a snowy white surplice, was the first to enter, followed by the village priest, who was, in turn, followed by a young boy carrying the royal crown on a white satin pillow. The crown, Noel had informed the Darlings, was seldom worn, since the weight of the gold and precious stones totaled more than four pounds.

Behind the crown marched a number of young boys, clad in the somber black-and-white garb of altar boys the world over. They were followed by the members of the Montacroix legislature, who were wearing red robes over their dark business suits. The prime minister was next, bearing a heavy mace encrusted with semiprecious stones. Dixie, reading from her tour book before the ceremony, had explained that the ornate mace represented the prince's delegated authority.

Everyone took their places on either side of the high throne at the front of the cathedral.

The music changed, heralding the arrival of the royal family. Prince Eduard, clad in a flowing purple robe, and Jessica, wearing a beaded ivory gown and a dazzling display of royal jewels, led the Giraudeau procession down the red carpet. The prince was breaking with tradition by having his wife at his side rather than making her follow submissively behind him, Dixie whispered to Sabrina, her approval obvious.

Chantal was next, accompanied by Caine. Bringing up the rear of the procession was Noel. The family climbed the five carpeted steps to stand in front of the altar.

An expectant hush settled over the vast building.

And then, the door at the back of the cathedral opened again, and on a grand flourish of trumpets, Prince Burke Giraudeau de Montacroix entered the cathedral.

His expression was more serious than Sabrina had ever seen it. Once more she was reminded of his deep, unwavering commitment to his country and his family and his duty. Despite the fact that Chantal was beaming, Sabrina noticed that her eyes glistened with happy tears. As did Noel's.

The coronation continued exactly as it had that first time, nearly two hundred years ago. The bishop gave his blessing to the proceedings, as did the priest. Then the bishop, assisted by the village priest and altar boys, offered a mass. After the royal family and the assembled spectators received communion, the bishop offered a closing prayer.

And then, finally, the moment everyone had been waiting for arrived. The prime minister rose from his gilt chair, took the heavy jeweled gold crown from its satin bed, placed it atop Eduard's head, then bent down on one knee, accepting the prince as his sovereign.

That was the cue for Burke, who had been standing on the sidelines, to approach and kneel before his father.

Another hush fell over the cathedral as Eduard stood, lifted the ornate crown from his head, held it high, allowing all assembled to view it. Then finally, with deliberate, theatrical slowness, he placed the crown upon his son's dark head.

A collective sigh of relief rippled through the room. Prince Burke was regent; the time for rebellion had passed.

Burke rose and bowed, first to his father, then his mother, then the legislators. The prime minister returned his bow and handed him the symbolic mace.

As Burke turned and bowed to the assembled spectators, the solemn stillness was spectacularly broken by the brassy clangor of the twelve bells in the cathedral belfry sending their heart-lifting song out across the Montacroix countryside.

It was official. Montacroix had a new prince.

"I DON'T BELIEVE IT!" Ariel stared when Sabrina joined her sisters and mother in the living room of the suite. "Please tell me you're not really planning to wear that monstrosity."

"This monstrosity, as you so unflatteringly put it, is sculpture," Sabrina shot back, admittedly defensive. She'd been hoping that the gown she'd maxed out her charge card for would improve with a second look. Unfortunately it hadn't.

"That dress is a nightmare," Raven countered. "You look like Batman in drag."

"I do not!"

"You do too. All you're missing is the mask and the Batmobile."

"If you're trying to turn Burke off, you're certainly goin' about it in the right way," Ariel declared. "That dress makes a nun's habit look downright sexy."

"Now girls," Dixie said, quickly stepping in to referee, as she'd done so many times when they were children, "leave Sabrina alone. I think she looks..." Her voice drifted off as she struggled to find something complimentary to say. "Very original!" She sent a sharp, warning look Ariel and Raven's way.

"I bought it from a boutique Chantal recommended," Sabrina said as they left the suite.

"Either the princess is fond of practical jokes, or some sadistic saleswoman saw you coming," Raven said.

Still torn with indecision, Sabrina didn't answer. Finally, when they reached the bottom of the stairs, Dixie turned to her and said, "You know, dear, there's time for you to change before the first waltz."

A gilt-framed mirror hung on a nearby silk-draped wall. One glance into it and Sabrina made her decision. "I think I will. You all go along to the ballroom without me," she said. "I'll be along as soon as I can."

"Wear that beaded red dress you wore onstage in Dallas," Dixie suggested. "The one that made all those cowboys go wild."

Sabrina didn't point out that was exactly why she'd bought this voluminous widow's weed in the first place. She didn't want to appeal to any more cowboys. What she wanted was to appear to be, if only for one night, as sophisticated and chic as all those European princesses Burke was accustomed to.

Deciding that the gold dress she wore to the casino would have to suffice, Sabrina had just reached the door to the suite when she heard voices.

"You missed your chance," Monique was saying. "Prince Burke is now regent. Montacroix remains a monarchy."

"Not for long," a male voice responded. "It was too risky to make another attempt on his life during the festival or the coronation. But now that he's been crowned, his protectors are bound to relax their guard."

"You hope," Monique spat back.

"I know. When the prince descends the staircase to enter the ballroom tonight, that will be his first and final appearance as regent."

Sabrina pressed her hand over her mouth to stifle her gasp. Intending to run and warn the others of the assassination attempt, she spun around and found herself face to face with a man who seemed strangely familiar.

"Your mother should have taught you better manners, mademoiselle." The man's gloved fingers curled around her arm. "It is impolite to eavesdrop."

"Eavesdrop?" Sabrina flashed him a bright smile, hoping to give the performance of her life. "I don't know what you're talking about. I only came back to my room in order to change my dress."

"Nice try." His fingers tightened, pressing deeply and painfully into her flesh. "But I'm afraid that your innocent act needs a bit more polish."

He opened the door, revealing Monique and another man Sabrina recognized to be one of the two liveried doormen who'd greeted the limousine her first day in Montacroix.

"What are you doing here?" the maid spat at Sabrina, her tone worlds different from the submissive attitude that had grated so on Sabrina's nerves.

"Don't be so unfriendly," the man who held Sabrina chided Monique. "As it is, this charming American actress has provided us with a new scenario." He ran his leather-clad hand down Sabrina's throat. "We now have a pretty bird in the hand."

Monique shook her head. "What does that mean?"

"It means, my thickheaded little aristocratic twit,"

the man said tightly, "that rather than meet the prince on his own turf, we will use his mistress to lure him into a trap."

"Oh." Monique's eyes brightened, giving her the look of a child who's just discovered a pretty new doll beneath the Christmas tree. "I like that!"

"I thought you would," the man agreed. "Especially since Prince Burke declined your father's suggestion that he link two old families by marriage."

Monique tossed her hair over her shoulder with arrogant female disdain. "I wouldn't have the prince if he crawled over broken glass."

"That's what they all say," the man agreed on a deep guttural laugh. He returned his attention to Sabrina, who was struggling valiantly for calm. She'd belatedly recognized him as the man she'd seen on the street after leaving the casino.

"You look as if you're feeling a bit faint, my dear." He ran the back of his leather glove down her pale cheek. "It must be all the excitement." He handed her over to the doorman. "Why don't you escort the lady outside for a breath of fresh air?"

The young man grinned and gave Sabrina a deep, mocking bow. "Mademoiselle, it would be my pleasure." He pressed a gun against her side. "Now be a good girl," the traitorous doorman advised, "and you will not be harmed."

Sabrina didn't believe him for a minute. When their attempt to kill Burke failed—and it was unthinkable to believe that it wouldn't—they couldn't risk allowing a witness to remain alive.

"And you've got a bridge you want me to buy, too, right?"

A look of puzzlement moved across his handsome features. "I do not understand the reference."

"Forget it."

The doorman currently on duty snapped to attention when Sabrina approached. Sabrina was tempted to try to break free and scream for help, but unwilling to endanger the life of an innocent man—a man who had just yesterday proudly shown her pictures of his children—she held her tongue.

"Mademoiselle Darling was feeling a bit faint," her captor said, pushing her through a clutch of formally dressed guests who had just arrived. "I'm taking her out for some air. Prince Burke's orders."

"Of course," the man agreed without missing a beat. He nodded his prematurely gray head. "You look, uh, very lovely tonight, as always, mademoiselle."

Sabrina saw the lie in his eyes and once again wondered what had made her buy such a bleak and unfeminine dress. It was all Burke's fault, she decided with a quick rush of temper. He'd muddled her mind so she couldn't even think straight.

"Thank you, Kirk," she murmured unenthusiastically.

Before she'd won the role of Maggie the Cat, Sabrina had played a troubled young woman who attempted suicide after a disastrous love affair with a married man. At the time, she hadn't completely understood why her character, who'd moped around in baggy black sweats for two acts, had donned her most alluring nightgown before swallowing all those pills.

Now Sabrina understood the character's motives all too well. One thing was certain. She was damned if she was going to be found dead in this stupid bat gown.

BURKE DIDN'T ATTEMPT to conceal his disappointment when the Darling family arrived at the ball without Sabrina.

"Where is she?" he asked after greeting Dixie, who'd joined the long line of individuals wanting to congratulate him on his coronation.

Dixie didn't pretend not to understand who Burke was referring to. "She'll be along later," she assured him. "She just wanted to change her dress. So she'd look pretty for you."

"Sabrina would look beautiful in whatever gown she was wearing." Or not wearing, Burke considered.

"I wouldn't be so sure of that," Ariel said silkily.

Before Burke could respond, Noel broke out of the receiving line and rushed over to him. "Burke, there's something wrong with Sabrina."

At the same time, a crackling came from beneath Caine's tuxedo jacket. He pulled out the walkie-talkie. "Yeah?"

Burke watched his brother-in-law and sister exchange a knowing glance and felt his heart lurch. "What is it?"

"They've taken Sabrina hostage," Caine revealed. "But my man's on their tail."

"Where is she at this moment?"

"In the rose garden," Noel and Caine answered in unison.

As he raced from the ballroom, creating a murmur of startled complaints from the guests still waiting their turn to speak with him, Burke vowed that when Sabrina was safe—and he could not allow himself to think that she would not be—he would not give her up.

12

As SABRINA was being dragged through the garden, her flowing dress caught on one of Jessica's prized rosebushes, bringing her to an abrupt halt.

"Quit stalling," her captor ground out. He nearly jerked her arm out of her socket. "We must get off the grounds before you are discovered missing."

"I'm not stalling, dammit." Sabrina tugged on the black crepe. "My stupid skirt is caught on all these thorns."

Cursing, he leaned down and yanked viciously, tearing off her skirt in a ragged line just below her knees.

"Now look what you've done!" Forgetting all about his deadly gun, Sabrina turned on him. "Do you have any idea how much this dress cost? You owe me!"

"So sue me." Unfazed by her female fury, he jerked her forward by the front of the dress, ripping it to the waist.

"Okay! That's it." Furious at being manhandled, and angered that now she wasn't even going to be able to return the hideous gown for a refund, Sabrina shoved him back.

Not expecting an assault from his captive, the man was caught off guard. And off balance. He stumbled backward, into a towering bush. The many-petaled, scarlet blossoms, protected by long vicious thorns, had been named for Princess Chantal.

The man cursed violently as those thorns ripped at

his muscled arms and handsome face. The gun disappeared into the leafy green foliage.

He was struggling to get to his feet when Sabrina caught sight of a garden rake, fortuitously left behind by an absentminded gardener. The man saw the rake at the same instant and dived for it, but Sabrina was faster. She scooped it up and held it over him, the steel tines gleaming in the moonlight.

"Don't even think about moving," she warned. "Or those scratches on your face are going to get a lot deeper." She waved the rake threateningly. "I see some rust. I do hope you've had a tetanus shot recently."

His only answer was a string of pungent curses and uncomplimentary references to Sabrina's parentage.

"Tsk, tsk," she murmured, even as she tried to figure out how she was going to extricate herself from what was still a very sticky situation. "For a so-called aristocrat, you certainly don't have very good manners. My mother always told me that cussing was an indication of an insufficient vocabulary."

That earned her even more curses, along with some deadly, uncomfortably specific threats. Sabrina wished she knew where the gun had landed. She didn't know how long she could manage to hold him off with merely a rusty garden rake.

As her eyes scanned the moist earth, looking for the weapon, she caught sight of the material he'd ripped from the hem of her dress.

"Here." She scooped up the black strip of cloth and flung it at him. "Tie yourself up."

"What?" He looked at her as if she'd just grown another head.

"I said, tie yourself up."

"You must be joking!"

"In case you hadn't noticed, buster, this isn't really a joking matter. Tie that around your ankles. Then I'll take care of your wrists."

"Sorry, baby," he growled. "You're cute, but I'm not into bondage games."

His nasty tone, along with his sexual innuendo, did nothing to quell her frustration about the fact that what should have been the most romantic night of her life was turning out to be a nightmare.

After all, how many times in one life did an average woman get to attend a royal ball? The way Sabrina looked at it, tonight was her one chance. And this stupid miscreant was spoiling it for her!

"I said, tie the damn cloth around your ankles!" She swung the rake, just missing his head when he ducked in the nick of time.

"*Merde!* All right, all right." His hands were visibly shaking as he wrapped the black crepe around his legs.

"That's better." She gestured with the rake again. "Now roll over onto your stomach and put your hands behind your back."

To her amazement, he did as instructed. Then, cautiously, she knelt beside him, took both ends of the remaining cloth, looped it around his wrists and tugged, drawing his legs up to his back.

She'd just finished when Burke, accompanied by Caine and a surprising number of armed men, came tearing around the corner.

"Well, if it isn't the cavalry," Sabrina said, greeting her would-be rescuers with a welcoming grin. "Just in the nick of time."

"Peterson here was right on your tail," Caine said, gesturing toward the other doorman.

"But I got lost in the damn maze," the former U.S.

government agent admitted, his tone tinged with self-loathing.

Feeling a rush of relief so strong it weakened his knees, Burke pulled Sabrina to her feet and held her tightly against him.

"From the very first, I thought you were a woman for whom any man would willingly fight hordes of fire-breathing dragons." He brushed a tender kiss against her temple. "I should have known that you would insist on slaying your own dragons."

Had ever a man's arms felt so good? So right? Sabrina tilted her head back and pressed her palm against his cheek, as if to convince herself that he was really there.

"He ruined my dress," she said, as if by way of explanation.

Reluctant to release her, even for a moment, Burke put her a little away from him and flicked his dark eyes over the lush, feminine body he'd come to know so well.

"I can't see that is much of a loss," he said finally.

Not about to protest such an accurate statement, Sabrina laughed. "Probably not," she agreed. "But it cost me nearly three months' rent."

"Don't worry." Burke ran his hand down her hair. "The court will make the perpetrators pay for your dress." And so long as she promised to stay away from black, he would buy her a hundred—a thousand—dresses, Burke vowed silently.

The walkie-talkie crackled again. "Drew's picked up Monique and our would-be assassin," Caine revealed. "The guy's not talking, but Monique is proving an absolute font of information."

Burke thought about the lovely, aggressive young woman who, only last year, had attempted to seduce him in an attempt to become queen. He'd always known her family had French ties. Obviously they'd been stronger than either he or his father had realized.

Both families were waiting for them at the palace. Eduard was, characteristically, furious. His wife and daughters expressed grave concern and sympathy. As did Ariel and Raven. Dixie took one look at Sabrina's disheveled state and began to bawl.

It took some time to assure everyone that she was all right. Finally, once Dixie's tears had slowed to a torrent, Chantal drew Sabrina aside.

"I see you let Françise bully you," she murmured, her brown eyes taking in the tattered gown.

"She ran me down like a bulldozer."

"Don't, as you Americans say, feel like the Lone Ranger," Chantal said. "She used to do the same thing to me. You've no idea how many horrid designer gowns I ended up giving away to charity auctions before I learned to stand up to her."

She patted Sabrina's muddy arm. "Don't worry. Before Caine and I return to Washington, I shall give you lessons on how to deal with her."

Before Sabrina could point out that she wasn't going to have any further dealings with the opinionated boutique owner, Chantal had turned toward her brother.

"Shouldn't you be getting back to the ball, Burke? You did, after all, leave the Prince of Wales standing in the receiving line."

When Burke looked at Sabrina, clearly torn between duty and love, Chantal made a shooing motion with her beringed hand.

"Go," she insisted. "Sabrina needs a bath and a change of clothes. We'll be along shortly."

Reluctantly bowing to duty, Burke stunned Sabrina and pleased everyone else present by pulling her into his arms and giving her a long, heartfelt kiss that left no question how he felt.

"Don't be too long," he murmured against her lips. "Because the party can't start without you."

And then he was gone, attending to his royal obligations, as Sabrina understood he must. But as she followed Chantal up the curving staircase, she pressed her fingertips against her lips and imagined she could still feel the heat of Burke's kiss.

THE BALL WAS every romantic fantasy, every youthful daydream, every dazzling fairy tale come to life.

To Sabrina's surprise and pleasure, Burke threw royal protocol to the wind, dancing every dance with her. And although she knew such uncharacteristically selfish behavior from Montacroix's new regent was seen by some as scandalous—most particularly those European beauties who were eyeing her with undisguised resentment—Sabrina didn't care.

Because as she waltzed in Burke's arms, Sabrina felt as if she were floating on air.

"I knew it," he murmured as he drew her closer and brushed a kiss against her hair.

"Knew what?" Her voice was soft and dreamy.

"That you'd be a marvelous dancer." She fit so perfectly into his arms. His bed. His life. "You seem to float."

She tilted her head back and smiled up at him. "That's because my feet haven't touched the ground for hours." She was, indeed, in seventh heaven.

With a deft skill he glided her toward the edge of the vast ballroom floor and out a pair of open French doors onto a brick terrace.

"People will talk," she demurred. As grateful as she was for any time alone with Burke before her flight left tomorrow morning, Sabrina was dreading the inevitable conversation yet to come.

This night, which had begun so horridly, was turning out to be the most magical, the most heavenly night of her life. Reality would be a most unwelcome intrusion.

"Let them talk." Because he needed to, because he'd been going crazy holding her in his arms all night without kissing her, Burke lowered his mouth to hers.

Sweet. She tasted so sweet. Burke knew that he could live a hundred—a thousand—years, and never tire of the taste of Sabrina's soft lips.

Her eyes opened slowly, reluctantly, when their lips finally parted. Desire had clouded her mind, causing her to forget to censure her words.

"I could spend the rest of my life like this," she murmured, her hands linked around his neck, her fingers playing with the soft ebony waves at the back of his nape. "Kissing you in the moonlight."

He rocked forward on the balls of his feet and touched his mouth to her softly smiling one. "Or in the sunshine," he suggested. He traced the outline of her upturned lips with the tip of his tongue, rewarded by her slight tremor. "Or the rain."

The thought of making love to Sabrina in a Montacroix summer rain, kissing the warm moisture from every inch of fragrant female skin, made his body quicken.

Pressing against him, Sabrina felt his hard arousal and shared his need. One glance over his shoulder at the crowded ballroom reminded her all too vividly that they were not alone.

Slipping out of his arms, she walked the few steps over to the balustrade and looked out over the rose garden. Had it only been three hours ago that she'd been in danger of losing her life in that fragrant maze? It seemed like an eternity. Another lifetime.

It seemed, Sabrina considered, that it had happened to some other woman.

Burke looked at her standing in the moonlight and decided that first thing in the morning, he was going to find a painter to capture the arresting image for his bedroom wall. The thought of being able to wake up every morning to the sight of his bride, looking ethereally sensual, was definitely appealing.

He came to stand behind her. "Have I told you that you look exceptionally beautiful tonight, *ma chérie?*"

She leaned back against him. "Several times. But don't let that stop you from telling me again." She sighed happily. "A woman never tires of hearing that the man she—" She hesitated when the word *loves* almost slipped out. "When the man she cares for," she continued, "finds her attractive."

He caught her hesitation and chose to overlook it. Instead, turning her in his arms, he smiled down at her and said, "I could tell you how lovely you are every minute of every day and it would not be enough."

The remarkable thing, Sabrina determined, looking up into his warm dark eyes, was that Burke meant it. Never before had she felt so appreciated. Never before had she felt so loved.

And suddenly, never had she felt so miserable. "I think I know exactly how Cinderella felt," she murmured. Midnight was coming. All too soon.

She brushed her nervous hands over her skirt, a gossamer, silvery, ice blue confection, studded with thousands of crystal beads that glittered like fallen stars in the slanting silver moonlight.

The dress belonged to Chantal. As the princess had pulled it from her closet and pushed it into Sabrina's arms, she'd explained how she'd bought it on an expensive whim, only to discover that the shimmering hue did nothing for her dark coloring.

She hadn't known why she saved the dress, Chantal had admitted. Until now. The dazzling, one-of-a-kind gown had been designed, she'd insisted, with Sabrina in mind.

Standing in front of the princess's floor-length mirror, staring in awe at the exquisite vision that was her own reflection, Sabrina had to admit Chantal was right.

Her belief had been seconded by the hot male admiration she'd seen in Burke's midnight dark eyes when she'd entered the ballroom.

It was the same look he was giving her now. That wonderful, hungry look that possessed the power to melt her bones. At the moment, knowing how this night must end, the warm gaze was making her increasingly nervous.

Sabrina sought something, anything, to say. "Your sister makes a terrific fairy godmother." Her laugh was thin and shaky. She plucked at the floaty, billowing skirt with nerveless fingers. "I almost expected her to pull out a pair of glass slippers."

"I've heard that glass slippers are extremely uncomfortable." Burke felt the fanciful, romantic mood slipping away, like drifting moon dust between his fingers. "They're also impossible to dance in."

The time had come. He'd put it off too long.

Drawing her back into his arms, he said, "I love you, Sabrina."

It was what she'd been waiting all her life to hear. It was what she'd been dreading for days. She tried to speak, but her mind, which earlier had been filled with all the sane, practical reasons why she and Burke could not have a future together, went completely blank. She could only stare up at him.

She'd gone rigid in his arms. Her soft eyes, which had been gazing at him all night with vivid, uncensored love, shadowed with something that inexplicably appeared to be fear.

"I love you," he repeated slowly, purposefully. "And I want you to be my wife."

Music was floating on the soft night air; Sabrina imagined she could hear the strident sound of the palace clock striking twelve.

Pulling free of his light touch, she backed away. "This is a mistake."

His body was hyperventilating, but Burke managed, just barely, to keep his growing desperation from showing. "On the contrary. The reason I've never asked a woman—any woman—to marry me before is because, having witnessed the love my father and stepmother shared, I did not want to make a mistake."

He moved slowly, purposefully toward her. Sabrina kept backing up until her beaded skirt was pressed up against the stone balustrade.

Burke framed her pale face between his palms and gave her a long look that was meant to reassure. "This is not a mistake."

"Yes." She closed her eyes and prayed for strength. "It is. Because I can't be what you want me to be."

"I love you." He said the words as if they were all that mattered.

Sabrina wished they were. "That's not enough."

"Of course it is." His low tone was calm and sure, reminding her that Eduard and Chantal weren't the only ones in the family possessing the Giraudeau tenacity. Prince Burke possessed it as well. In spades.

"Oh, Burke." She sighed, her gaze misting as she

looked up at him. "I'd make a miserable wife. I have a terrible temper, I can be horrendously moody, you'd never know who you were living with because I have a horrible habit of becoming whatever character I'm playing, sometimes I'll go an entire week without hanging up my clothes—"

"I love you."

She wasn't getting through. Finally, desperate, Sabrina took a deep breath and said, "I can't have children."

She watched the shock move across his handsome face in waves. Then, she had to admire the speed with which he recovered.

"Can't?" he inquired on that same steady, reasonable tone. "Or won't?"

"Can't." The word hung between them, irrevocable and final. "I had an infection last year. Since I was performing five nights a week, along with Wednesday and Sunday matinees, I kept putting off making time to go to the doctor."

She dragged her hand through her hair and took a deep, shuddering breath. "When I finally collapsed on-stage, they rushed me to the hospital and performed emergency surgery."

His dark brow crashed down and he took her ice-cold hand in his. "You were in danger?"

He was getting off track, but she answered anyway. "I almost died."

He cursed. "I should have been there."

If he had been, Sabrina knew, she wouldn't have waited so long before seeking medical help. He would have cared enough to insist she go to the doctor. While Arthur, on the other hand, had impatiently brushed her symptoms aside, accusing her of being just another temperamental artist seeking attention.

"The doctors saved my life. But the operation left me unable to have children." There. She'd said it. Sabrina stood still, every nerve end poised for Burke's rejection.

"There are specialists."

"I've been to the best specialists in New York City. They all agree. I'm barren." Such an old-fashioned word, Sabrina thought. Such a hateful word. But unfortunately, it fit.

Once again Burke surprised her. "It doesn't matter," he decided implacably. "Because I love you."

"It does matter." The tears that had been threatening at the back of her lids broke free. "Dammit, don't you see? I can't give you an heir, Burke. And without an heir, Montacroix returns to France." Single-handedly, she would achieve that unwelcome goal the horrid cadre of rebels had failed to accomplish.

"I have one question."

"What?" She was crying openly now, tears spilling down her cheeks in shining wet ribbons.

"Do you love me?"

She knew the safe thing, the prudent thing, would be to lie. But Sabrina couldn't do it. Not after all they'd shared.

"Of course I do," she cried. "But don't you see? It's not enough." She couldn't—wouldn't—be responsible for the dissolution of a two-hundred-year-old monarchy.

Somewhere, deep inside her, a self-protective anger flared. "Besides, in case you have forgotten, I'm not some silly female with nothing to do but sit around, eating bonbons while waiting for Prince Charming to carry me off. I have a career, Burke. One I've worked damn hard to establish.

"And then there's the tour. What makes you think I

could just drop everything, leaving Dixie in the lurch, just because you had a whim for a royal wedding?''

Pushing past him, she raced down the stone steps, her beaded skirt billowing behind her. Burke didn't follow. Instead he stood there all alone in the dark, his arms folded across his chest and watched her run away.

He'd give her time to get used to the idea, Burke decided reluctantly. He would also permit her to finish this tour, which was so important to her father's honor.

But the day the Darling sisters gave their last performance, Sabrina Darling was going to be his.

Forever.

13

TWELVE WEEKS LATER, Sabrina stood on the stage of the Las Vegas casino, drinking in the audience applause. It was, finally, the last night of the tour. Although they'd fallen short in their goal to earn the entire three million dollars that the government had claimed Sonny owed, for some reason, at the last minute, the IRS auditors had proved remarkably agreeable, settling for what they had earned and marking their father's debt paid in full. An additional surprise had been the reversal of the ruling that the government could seize her parents' Tennessee farm.

As the shiny silver curtain closed for the last time and the enthusiastic audience began filing from the vast dinner theater, Sabrina knew she should be ecstatic.

During these past three months, her lingering anger toward her father for not being perfect had vanished, and she could accept the fact that Sonny Darling, like everyone else, including herself, was flawed.

Indeed, Sabrina no longer blamed him for leaving behind so many problems. Instead she remembered the warm and generous love he'd always had for his family and his friends.

So, her duty to her father done, tomorrow morning she'd return to New York to meet with a producer who wanted her to star in his new play.

The play, entitled *Command Performance*, was a marvelous modern romantic musical takeoff on the classic Cinderella tale, bound to garner accolades from both critics and theatergoers.

Her career was at a turning point; she knew this play would establish her as a credible actor, an actor with range. And, as a bonus, she'd even get to sing.

Still, Sabrina felt let down. She tried telling herself that the grinding nine months of the tour had left her depressed. But she knew the real reason was that she missed Burke. Horribly.

Raven joined Sabrina in the wings. Together they watched the last of the audience leave. "Well, that's that," Raven said. "We can all return to our own lives."

"I suppose so," Sabrina murmured unenthusiastically.

"Yep," Raven said, "this time tomorrow, Ariel will be in Hollywood, I'll be in Atlanta and Mom'll be back on the farm."

When Sabrina didn't comment, Raven gave her a long, considering look. "So, where are you going to be?"

"New York," Sabrina answered promptly. "You know I've got a meeting with that producer."

"I thought, perhaps you'd change your mind."

"Why on earth would I do that? It's a marvelous part."

"I thought you might prefer to take on another role."

Sabrina understood Raven's meaning all too well. "Whatever there was between Burke and me was over three months ago. In case you haven't noticed, I haven't heard a word from him."

"That's not exactly true," her mother's voice entered the conversation. Sabrina briefly closed her eyes, praying for patience, as Dixie and Ariel joined them. "What about the flowers that have been delivered before every show?"

"You and Raven and Ariel get flowers, too."

"True, but your arrangements are always larger," Ariel who noticed such things, correctly pointed out.

"And what about Sonny's collection?" Dixie asked.

The antique Western guns had begun arriving at the farm a week after the Darlings' departure from Montacroix. Yesterday, Dixie had received a call from the housekeeper that the Winchester, the last of the collection, had been delivered.

"That doesn't count," Sabrina argued. "When you called Montacroix and asked Burke if he was behind the purchases, he told you he bought them back because he valued family tradition."

"What's wrong with that?"

"Nothing." Sabrina shrugged her bare shoulders. "In fact, it just drives home the point that his own family traditions make it impossible for us to be together."

"Why, I do declare," Ariel drawled. "You are acting every bit as dim-witted as Katie Stuart, when she let me steal her husband. And all because having come from a family of sharecroppers, she didn't believe she was good enough to be the wife of a Georgia state senator."

"Read my lips," Sabrina said slowly, as if speaking to someone who did not understand her language, "*Southern Nights* is a soap opera. Not real life."

"Actually," Dixie considered thoughtfully, "lately, real life has seemed a lot messier than any daytime television drama." She patted Sabrina's arm comfortingly. "It was obvious to everyone that you and Burke were in love, darling."

"So," Raven said, "since boy loves girl and girl loves boy, what's the problem?"

"How about the little fact that I can't give him an heir?"

Sabrina had told her mother and sisters the truth about her condition the day they'd left Montacroix. Although they'd responded with sympathy—and anger at Arthur Longstreet—none of them had been able to convince her that her inability to have a child was not an insurmountable barrier.

"You told us Burke said it didn't matter," Ariel reminded her.

"It was the moonlight talking."

"From what I saw of the prince, I doubt if he's ever—in his entire life—uttered a word he didn't mean," Raven said.

"I don't want to talk about Burke anymore," Sabrina insisted. "And if you don't all mind, I think I'd like to be alone for a little while."

"Of course," Dixie answered quickly. A bit too quickly, Sabrina considered. "We'll be upstairs, in our suite." She gave her stepdaughter a hug overbrimming with maternal comfort. "Come along girls, you can help me pack. I don't know why I always save it until the last minute," she complained as the trio disappeared behind the rows of stage curtain.

Alone at last, Sabrina walked back onto the stage and stood there, staring out at the empty theater, remembering the heady sound of applause that had rocked the rafters.

This was where she belonged, she reminded herself firmly. Onstage. Not locked away in some gilded tower like Rapunzel.

"Wrong fairy tale, Sabrina," she muttered out loud, her voice echoing in the vast emptiness. Exhaling a long weary sigh, she turned to leave, when suddenly, the red velvet-draped doors at the back of the theater burst open.

"I don't believe it!"

Sabrina couldn't decide whether to laugh or to cry as Burke came galloping down the aisle on that same black stallion he'd ridden the day they'd made love in the gamekeeper's cottage.

"Good evening, milady," he greeted her as he reined the horse in just below the stage.

His wonderful, all-too-familiar deep voice shattered her last thought that this might be a hallucination, born of her desperate, lonely thoughts.

"You've obviously gone stark raving mad," Sabrina accused, even as her out-of-control heart sprouted gossamer wings.

"Mad about you," Burke agreed easily. He held out his arms for her perusal. "What do you think? Do I live up to your image of Prince Charming?"

Oh, he did. In fact, he surpassed every romantic daydream she'd ever had. "The horse is supposed to be white."

"Surely a remarkably talented performer such as yourself would have heard of literary license," Burke countered easily. His tone was mild, but as he took in the sight of Sabrina dressed in a strapless, beaded red gown that fit like a lover's caress, heat rose in his eyes.

"I also had to leave most of the shining armor at home." He placed a hand against his gleaming chest plate. "Men were a great deal smaller back in the good old days of the Round Table. And the helmet's impossible to see out of."

"You look very dashing," Sabrina assured him.

"That's exactly what I wanted to hear. You, of course, look as delectable as ever."

The feelings were there, so strong Sabrina was surprised that the air wasn't lit with electrical sparks. But even as she wanted to fling herself into his arms, to cover his handsome, smiling face with kisses, she reminded herself that nothing had changed.

"What are you doing here, Burke?" she asked softly.

"Living out a fantasy?"

"No, really."

Burke wondered why he thought this was going to be easy. Biting back a curse, he reached into the leather bag attached to his saddle and pulled out a thick long roll of paper.

"I wanted to bring you this, for one thing."

She bent down and took the papers. "Blueprints?"

"For the new theater that's being built on the banks of Lake Losange," he informed her. "In fact, I would have been here sooner, but I've been tied up with architects trying to get the place designed before the end of your tour. Congratulations, by the way, on retiring your father's debt."

"We came in five hundred thousand short," she allowed. "But for some reason…"

Her voice drifted off as comprehension dawned. Sabrina was tempted to look above her head for the glowing light bulb. "If you paid that money—"

"I would never do such a thing without asking your permission first," Burke interrupted.

The needle on that internal lie detector, which had gotten such a workout during her marriage, was practically going off the chart. "But you did do something."

"All right." Burke shrugged his armor-clad shoulders. "As it turned out, your government wanted very much to negotiate a banking treaty with Montacroix. When I explained that I was uncomfortable signing my name to a joint accord with a government who seems unable to reach a compromise with its own citizens, the IRS came to the belated, but wise conclusion that the penalties assessed on your father's estate were mistakenly extreme."

It was the same thing Dixie's new accountant had told them in the beginning. Unfortunately the IRS had remained firm and the accountant, while a partner in a nationwide firm, had not possessed Burke's clout.

"You mixed private and state business? For me?"

"For your family," Burke corrected. "I have grown quite fond of your sisters and your mother."

"Thank you."

"It was my pleasure." Actually, Burke had rather enjoyed watching those State Department officials coming down so hard on the individuals who'd given Sabrina and her mother and sisters so much unwarranted grief.

"You still haven't looked at the drawings," he reminded her.

Her eyes skimmed over the drawings. The theater had been designed specifically for those small, intimate audiences that had made the Broadway theaters so special. "It looks very nice."

"I was hoping you'd think so. Of course, you're invited to make any changes you want. Look at the name," he suggested.

Her eyes widened. "You named an entire theater after me?"

"Of course. I thought it only appropriate. You are intending to perform for your subjects, aren't you?"

"Burke, we've been through this before—"

"I rather thought," Burke said, deftly cutting off her planned refusal, "that you might like to debut your new play and the theater at the same time."

"My new play?" She tapped the blueprints against

her palm. "Don't tell me that you're behind that meeting I have tomorrow!"

She did not, Burke considered, appear pleased. "Actually, I am. Is there a problem?"

"Is there a problem?" Her temper flared. She waved the blueprints at him. "How about the little fact that I was led to believe that I'd been offered that part because of my talent?" And not, Sabrina considered furiously, because she'd been sleeping with a prince.

"The play was written with you in mind," Burke said. "It was also written before you and I met."

Having had one man manipulate her life, Sabrina was not prepared to allow Burke, no matter how much she loved him, do the same.

"Then how do you know about it?"

"The afternoon you and your sisters left Montacroix, the producer called the palace, hoping to talk with you. I took the call and informed him that your plane had already left. Then we had a long talk about you. And his offer. By the end of the conversation, he'd agreed to consider bringing the play to Montacroix."

Burke held out his hands. "Believe me, Sabrina, that was my only involvement in the matter. If you do not wish to debut the play in my country, I would accept your decision."

"Every actor wants to play the palace," she murmured the old theater axiom.

"Does that mean that you agree?"

"I don't know." Sabrina was truly torn. Her heart was screaming *yes! yes!* Her mind was reminding her that nothing had changed.

"Perhaps this will help you make up your mind." Burke reached into the leather bag again and pulled out another paper.

The piece of parchment was rolled and tied with a

slim red ribbon. Sabrina scanned the brief lines, then looked up at him with wide and wary, but hopeful eyes.

"The legislature has amended the Montacroix charter," Burke answered her unspoken question. "The male ascendancy clause stands. But an additional clause has been added to the original."

"Allowing for the heir to be adopted," Sabrina whispered, having to push the words past the lump in her throat.

"That's right." Tired of being so close to her without touching, Burke dismounted and leaped onto the stage with a deft grace that reminded Sabrina vaguely of Douglas Fairbanks. He already was wearing the armor; all he needed was a sword to make the image complete.

"Motherhood and fatherhood have very little to do with biology, *chérie*," he insisted quietly. Somberly. He wrapped his strong arms around her. His palms stroked her rigid back, encouraging her to relax. "All that matters is that you and I will love our children." He pressed a kiss against her hair, her temple. "As we love each other."

Finally, because it had been an aeon since he'd touched her, kissed her, Burke lowered his mouth to hers.

Her bones were melting. As was the block of ice she'd encased her heart in twelve long weeks ago. "You seem to have thought of everything," she said breathlessly when the wonderful kiss finally ended.

"Lord, I hope so. Oh, there is one more little thing." With a great deal of reluctance, Burke released her long enough to dig into the front pocket of his slacks.

"You know," Sabrina said, feeling remarkably light-hearted for the first time in months, "you're beginning to look a lot more like Santa Claus than Prince Charming."

Her smile faded from her lips, her mouth went dry as Burke handed her a black velvet box. She opened it, unable to hold in her gasp when she viewed the dazzling ring—a gleaming gray pearl surrounded by a glittering stardust of flawless diamonds set in brilliant platinum—lying on its bed of royal blue satin.

"Oh, Burke."

"It's made from stones taken from the crown."

She looked up at him, clearly surprised. "Your crown?"

Burke shrugged. "I had them replaced with paste. No one will ever miss them. Besides, the crown is an outdated symbol. I have no intention of wearing it again."

She remembered what he'd said about bringing Montacroix into the twenty-first century and realized that his behavior was in character. But still, to strip his family's royal symbol of its precious stones for her was a major act of faith. And love.

"I couldn't find a ring I felt suited you," Burke explained. "So, I decided to have one made up. One that reminds me of your eyes, after we make love."

He took the ring from its satiny bed. "I love you, Sabrina. More than life itself. And I will love our adopted children every bit as much as my parents have always loved my sisters and me. As much as yours loved you."

His gaze was warm, but to her amazement, Sabrina viewed a hint of something that resembled fear in their swirling dark depths.

"Please don't turn me down again, *chérie.* Because I'm not certain my not inconsiderable ego could withstand another buffeting."

Burke Giraudeau de Montacroix was all Sabrina's fairy-tale dreams come to life. But he was better. Much, much better. Because he was flesh and blood and most importantly, he possessed a very warm, generous and wonderfully loving heart.

"I love you, Burke." She held out her trembling hand, giving him her answer.

When he slipped the ring onto her finger, tears of joy filled her eyes. He kissed her again, a long kiss that rocked her with emotion. Then, before she knew what was happening, he'd swept her up in his arms and she found herself seated across the saddle in front of Burke on the gleaming black stallion.

"I have one more thing to ask," Burke murmured in her ear as they rode off together into the dazzling desert night.

"What's that?" There was no request that she would not willingly grant this man who'd proved to her that happy endings really were possible, after all.

"Do you think we could convince your sisters to sing at our wedding?"

Happier than she'd ever been in her life, Sabrina laughed. "I'd like to see you try and stop them."

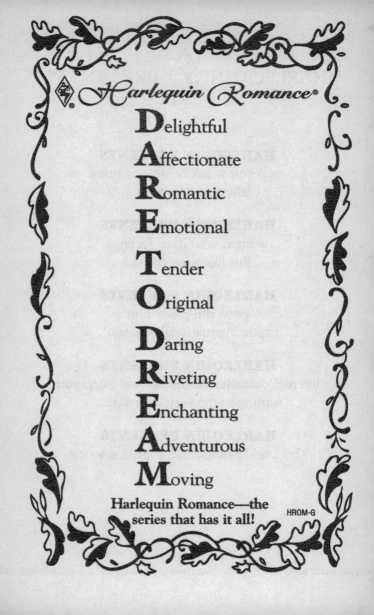

Harlequin Romance®

Dare to Dream

Delightful

Affectionate

Romantic

Emotional

Tender

Original

Daring

Riveting

Enchanting

Adventurous

Moving

Harlequin Romance—the
series that has it all!

HROM-G

HARLEQUIN PRESENTS®

HARLEQUIN PRESENTS
men you won't be able to resist
falling in love with...

HARLEQUIN PRESENTS
women who have feelings
just like your own...

HARLEQUIN PRESENTS
powerful passion in
exotic international settings...

HARLEQUIN PRESENTS
intense, dramatic stories that will keep you
turning to the very last page...

HARLEQUIN PRESENTS
The world's bestselling romance series!

Harlequin® Historical

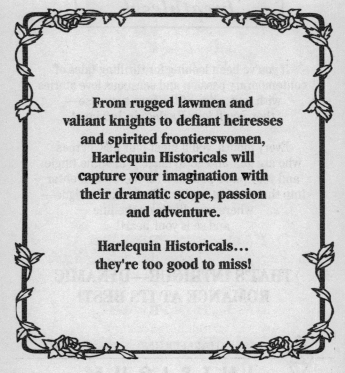

From rugged lawmen and
valiant knights to defiant heiresses
and spirited frontierswomen,
Harlequin Historicals will
capture your imagination with
their dramatic scope, passion
and adventure.

Harlequin Historicals...
they're too good to miss!

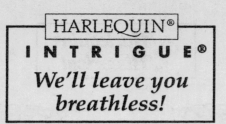

LOOK FOR OUR FOUR FABULOUS MEN!

Each month some of today's bestselling authors bring
four new fabulous men to Harlequin American Romance.
Whether they're rebel ranchers, millionaire power brokers
or sexy single dads, they're all gallant princes—and
they're all ready to sweep you into lighthearted fantasies
and contemporary fairy tales where anything is possible
and where all your dreams come true!

You don't even have to make a wish...
Harlequin American Romance will grant your every desire!

Look for Harlequin American Romance
wherever Harlequin books are sold!

HARLEQUIN SUPERROMANCE®

...there's more to the story!

Superromance. A *big* satisfying read about unforget-
table characters. Each month we offer
four very different stories that range from family
drama to adventure and mystery, from highly emotional stories to romantic comedies—and
much more! Stories about people you'll
believe in and care about. Stories too
compelling to put down....

Our authors are among today's *best* romance writ-
ers. You'll find familiar names and
talented newcomers. Many of them are
award winners—and you'll see why!

If you want the biggest and best
in romance fiction, you'll get it
from Superromance!

Available wherever Harlequin books are sold.

Look us up on-line at: http://www.romance.net

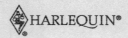

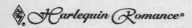

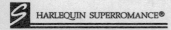

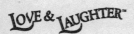

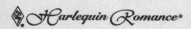

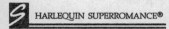

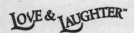